MORE PRAISE FOR BABYMOUSE!

"Sassy, smart . . .
Babymouse is here
to stay."
—The Horn Book Magazine

"Young readers
will happily
fall in line."
—Kirkus Reviews

"The brother-sister creative team hits the mark
with humor, sweetness, and characters so genuine
they can pass for real kids." —Booklist

"Babymouse is spunky, ambitious,
and, at times, a total dweeb."
—School Library Journal

D0035259

Be sure to read **all** the **BABYMOUSE** books:

#1 BABYMOUSE: Queen of the World!
#2 BABYMOUSE: Our Hero
#3 BABYMOUSE: Beach Babe
#4 BABYMOUSE: Rock Star
#5 BABYMOUSE: Heartbreaker
#6 CAMP BABYMOUSE
#7 BABYMOUSE: Skater Girl
#8 BABYMOUSE: Puppy Love
#9 BABYMOUSE: Monster Mash
#10 BABYMOUSE: The Musical
#11 BABYMOUSE: Dragonslayer
#12 BABYMOUSE: Burns Rubber
#13 BABYMOUSE: Cupcake Tycoon
#14 BABYMOUSE: Mad Scientist
#15 A Very BABYMOUSE Christmas
#16 BABYMOUSE for President
#17 EXTREME BABYMOUSE

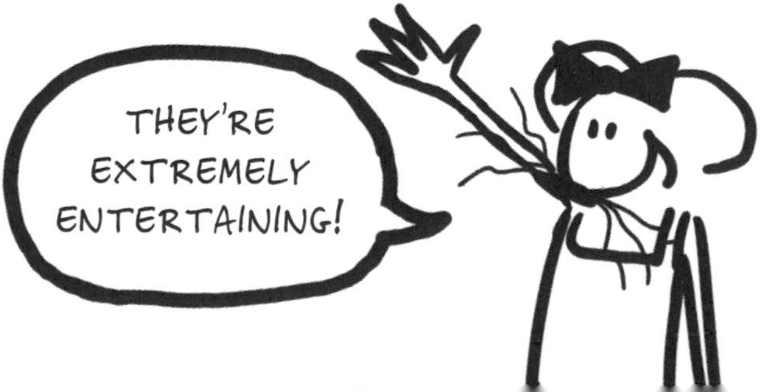
THEY'RE EXTREMELY ENTERTAINING!

EXTREME
BABYM♥USE

j
741.5
HOLM
2013

Walla Walla
County Libraries

BY JENNIFER L. HOLM & MATTHEW HOLM

RANDOM HOUSE 🏠 NEW YORK

THIS IS GONNA BE EXTREME!

EXTREMELY INTERESTING.

This is a work of fiction. All incidents and dialogue, and all characters with the exception of some well-known historical and public figures, are products of the authors' imagination and are not to be construed as real. Where real-life historical or public figures appear, the situations, incidents, and dialogues concerning those persons are fictional and are not intended to depict actual events or to change the fictional nature of the work. In all other respects, any resemblance to persons living or dead is entirely coincidental.

Copyright © 2013 by Jennifer Holm and Matthew Holm

All rights reserved. Published in the United States by Random House Children's Books, a division of Random House, Inc., New York.

Random House and the colophon are registered trademarks of Random House, Inc.

Special thanks to Jarrett Krosoczka for Lunch Lady's guest appearance.

Visit us on the Web!
randomhouse.com/kids
Babymouse.com

Educators and librarians, for a variety of teaching tools, visit us at RHTeachersLibrarians.com

Library of Congress Cataloging-in-Publication Data
Holm, Jennifer L.
Extreme Babymouse / by Jennifer L. Holm & Matthew Holm. — 1st ed.
  p. cm. — (Babymouse ; #17)
Summary: It seems that everyone at school has taken up snowboarding, so Babymouse decides she must hit the slopes, too.
1. Graphic novels. [1. Graphic novels. 2. Imagination—Fiction. 3. Snowboarding—Fiction. 4. Schools—Fiction.
5. Mice—Fiction.] I. Holm, Matthew. II. Title.
PZ7.7.H65Ext 2013 741.5'9—dc23 2012022834

ISBN 978-0-307-93160-3 (trade) — ISBN 978-0-375-97096-2 (lib. bdg.) — ISBN 978-0-307-97543-0 (ebook)

MANUFACTURED IN MALAYSIA   10 9 8 7 6 5 4 3 2 1   First Edition

Random House Children's Books supports the First Amendment and celebrates the right to read.

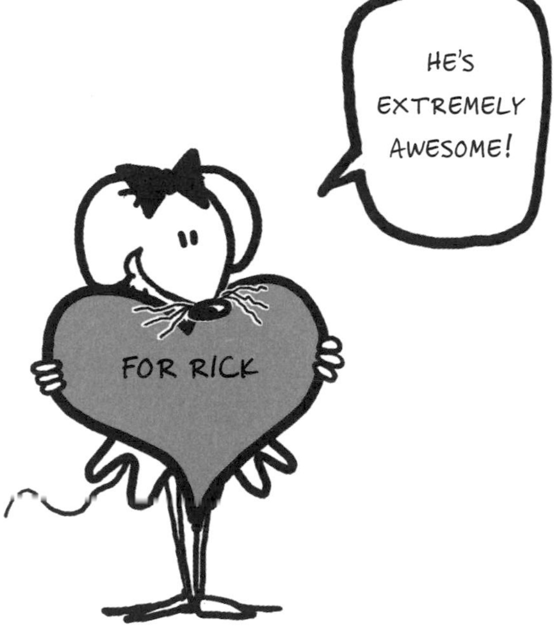
HE'S EXTREMELY AWESOME!
FOR RICK

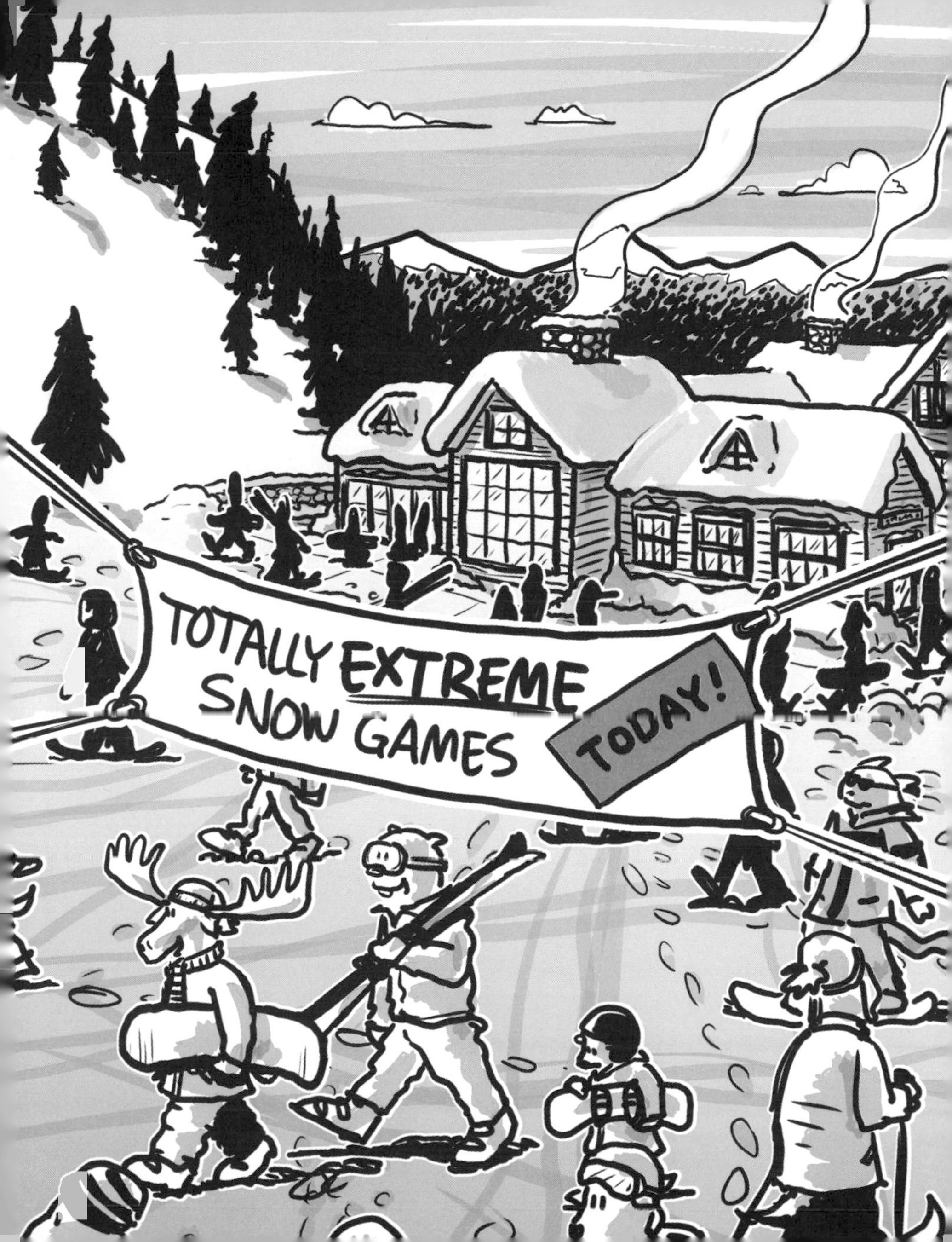
TOTALLY EXTREME
SNOW GAMES
TODAY!

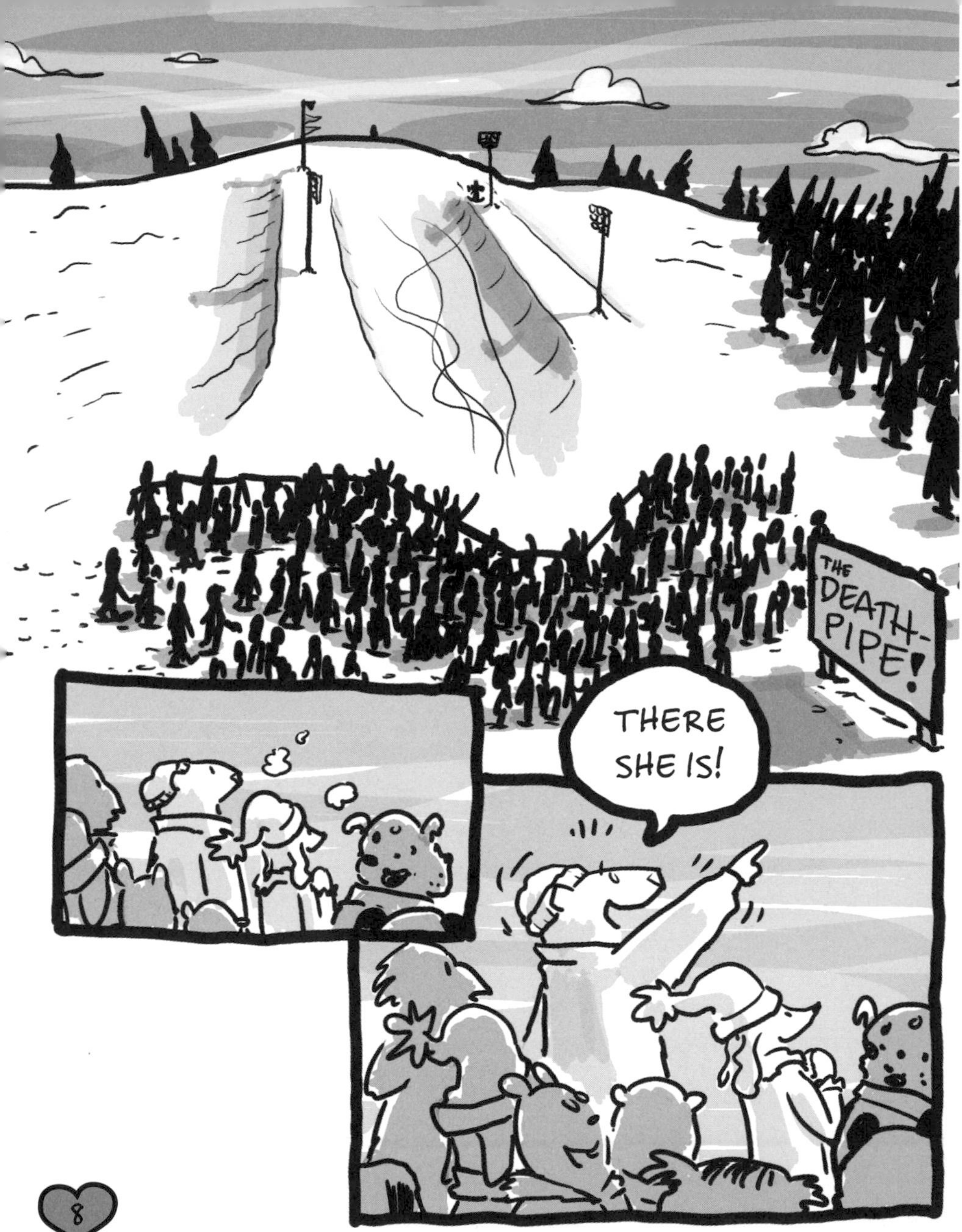
THE DEATH-PIPE!
THERE SHE IS!

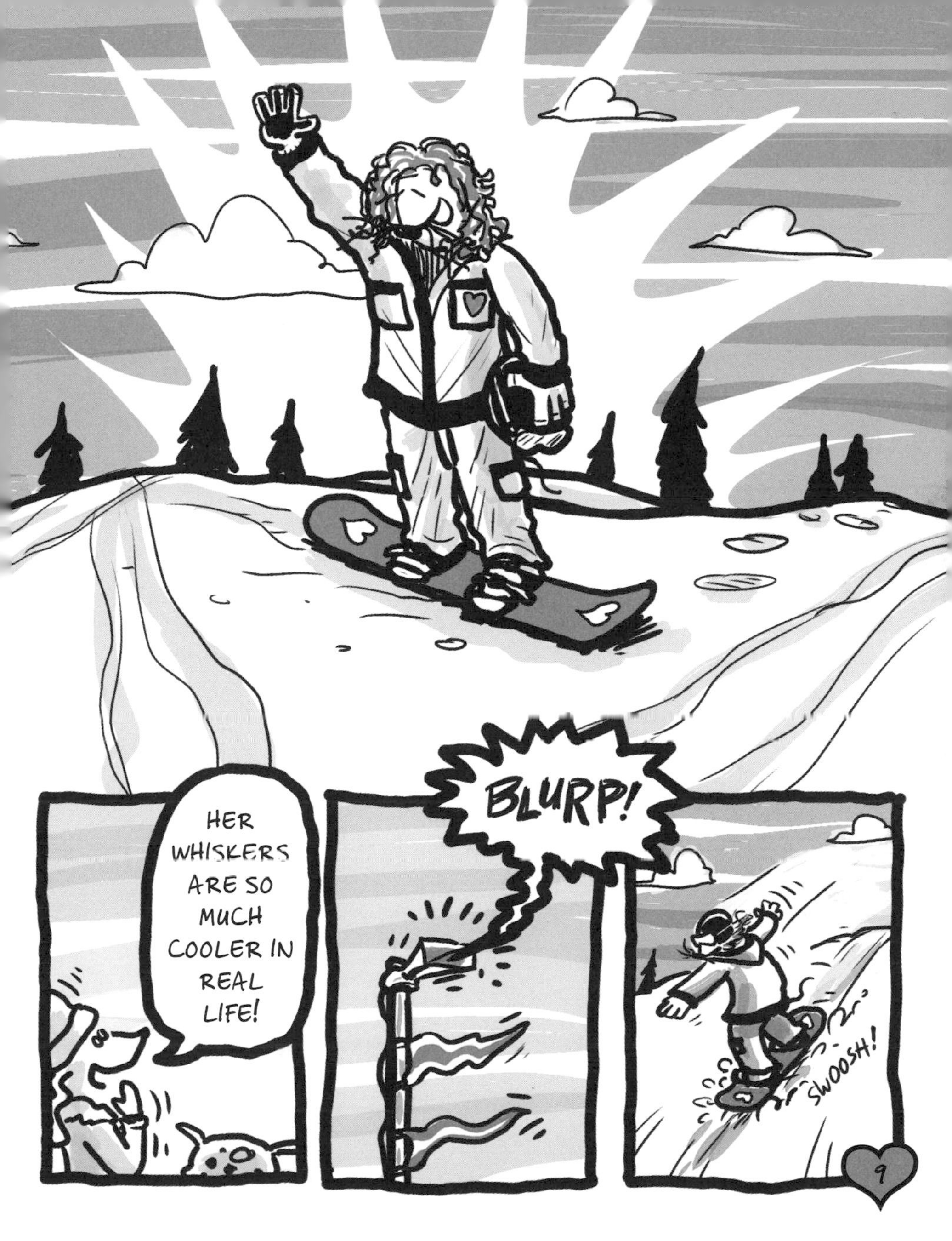
HER WHISKERS ARE SO MUCH COOLER IN REAL LIFE!
BLURP!
SWOOSH!

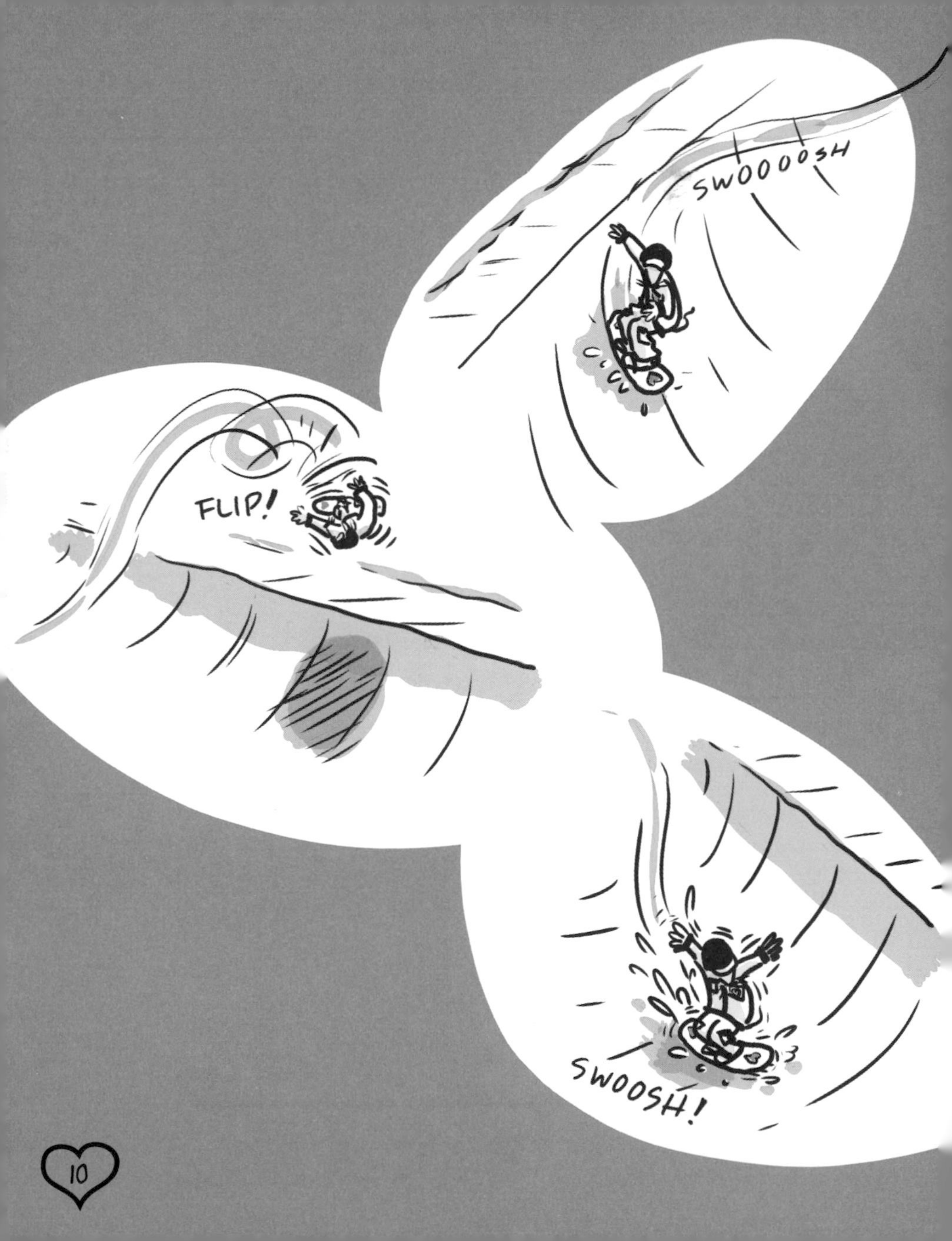
SWOOOOSH
FLIP!
SWOOSH!

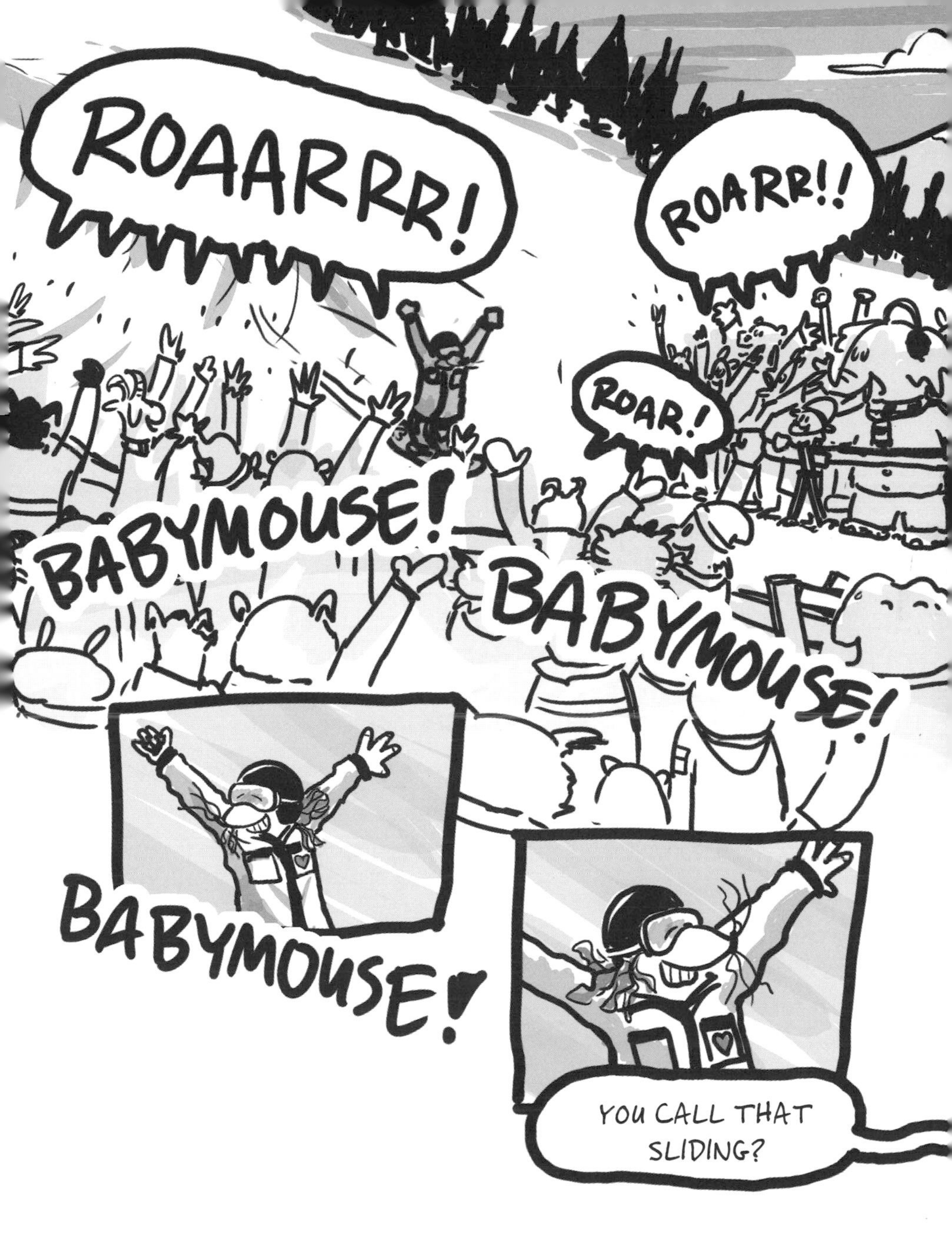
ROAARRR!
ROARR!!
ROAR!
BABYMOUSE!
BABYMOUSE!
BABYMOUSE!
YOU CALL THAT SLIDING?

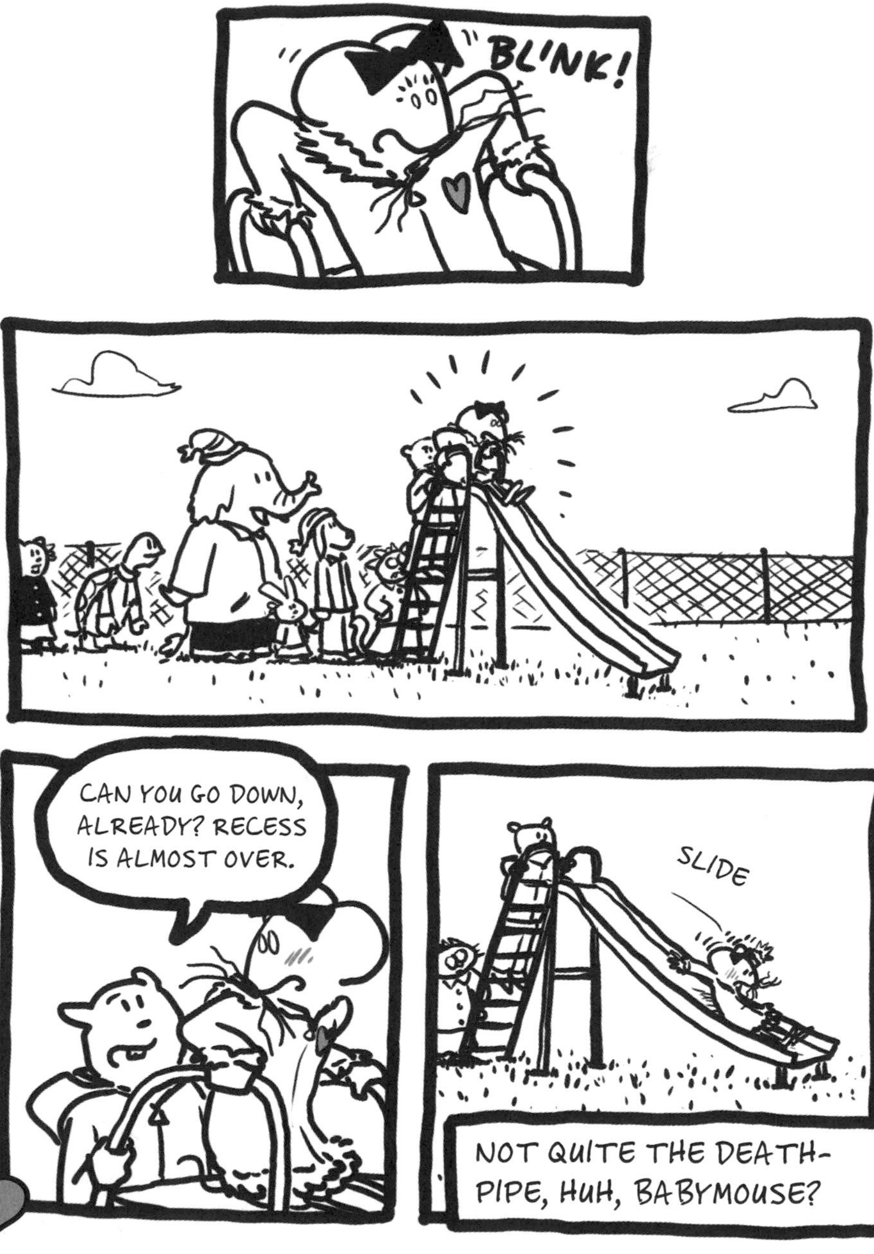
BLINK!
CAN YOU GO DOWN, ALREADY? RECESS IS ALMOST OVER.
SLIDE
NOT QUITE THE DEATH-PIPE, HUH, BABYMOUSE?

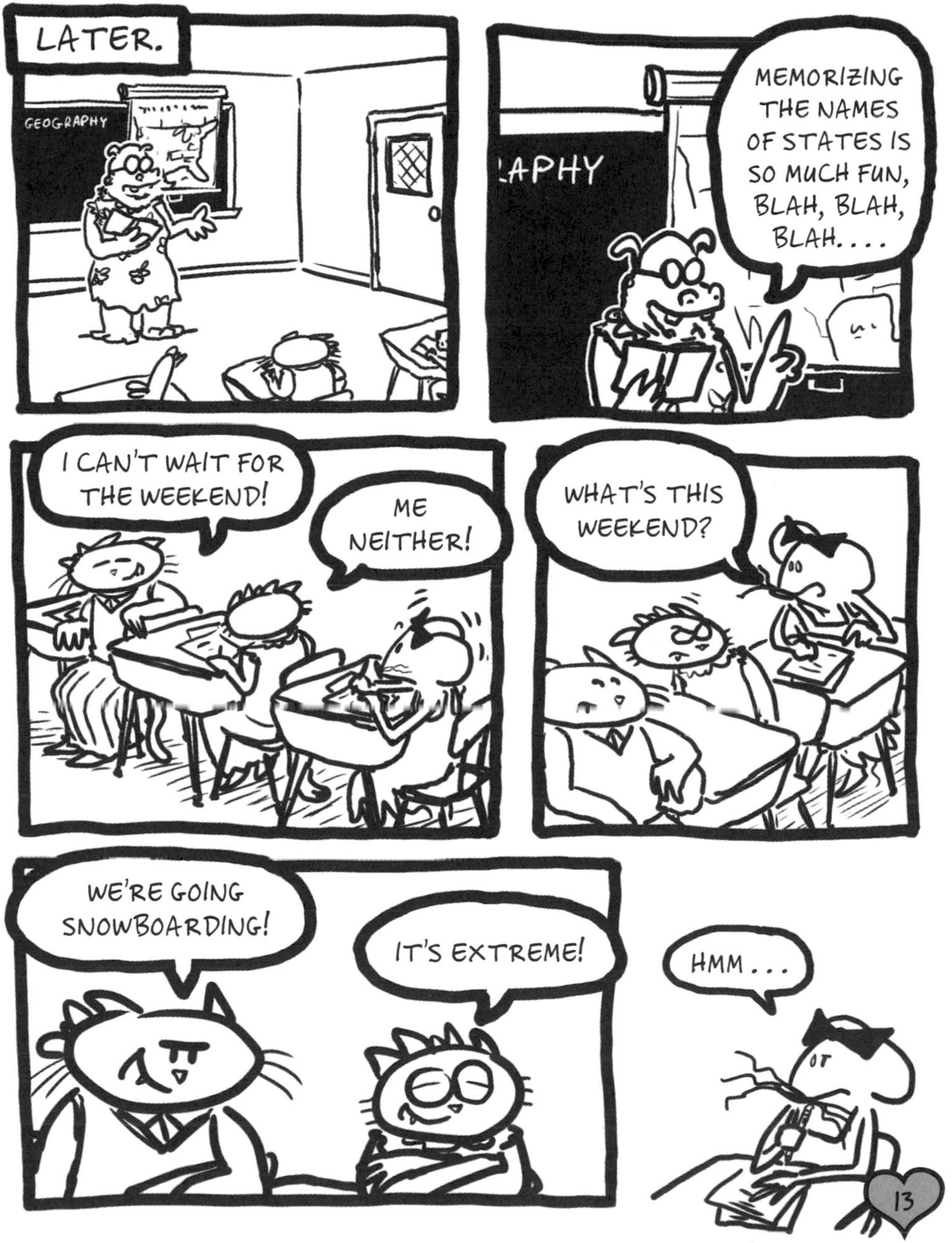

LATER.
GEOGRAPHY
MEMORIZING THE NAMES OF STATES IS SO MUCH FUN, BLAH, BLAH, BLAH. . . .
APHY
I CAN'T WAIT FOR THE WEEKEND!
ME NEITHER!
WHAT'S THIS WEEKEND?
WE'RE GOING SNOWBOARDING!
IT'S EXTREME!
HMM . . .

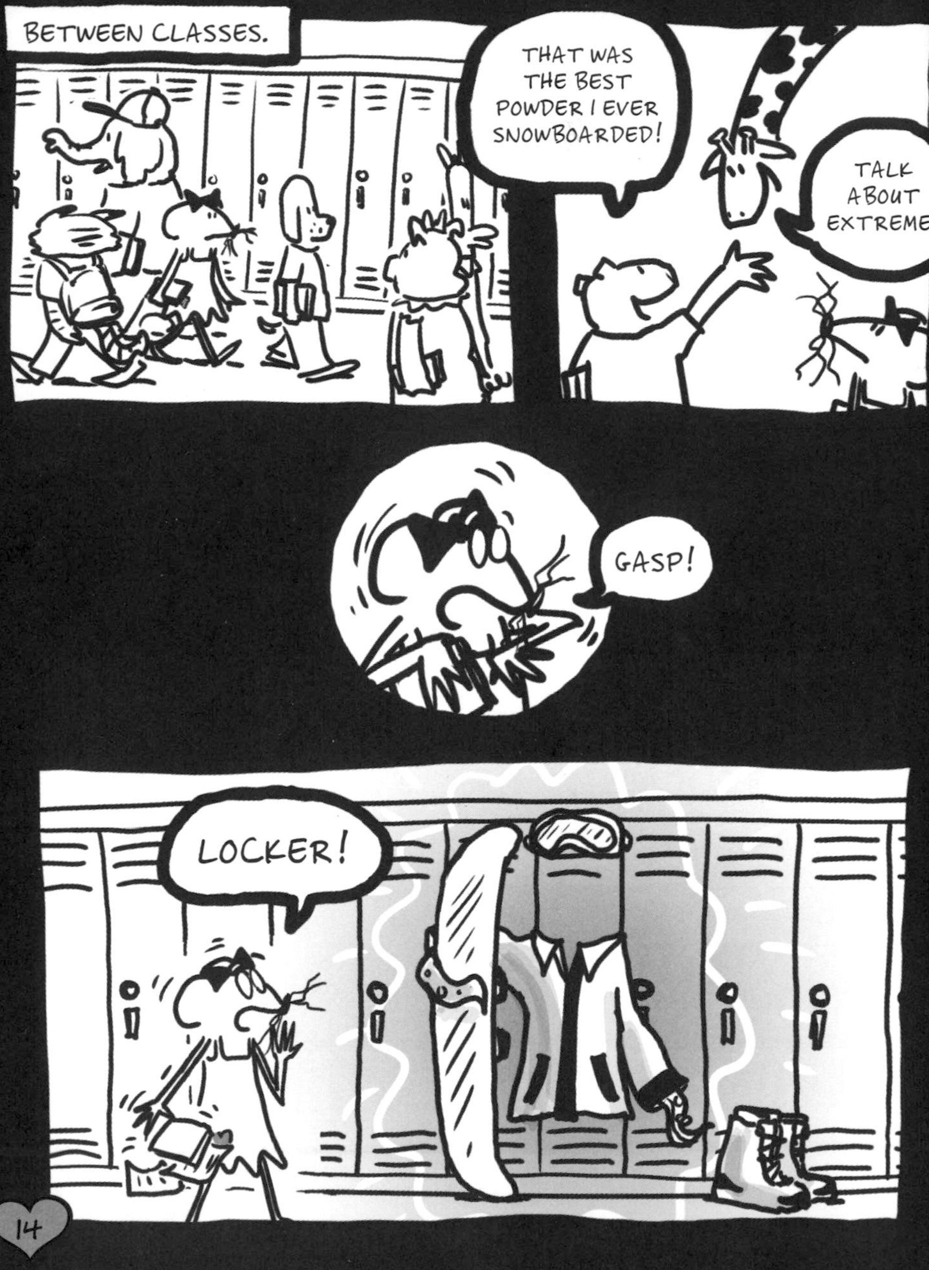
BETWEEN CLASSES.
THAT WAS THE BEST POWDER I EVER SNOWBOARDED!
TALK ABOUT EXTREME!
GASP!
LOCKER!

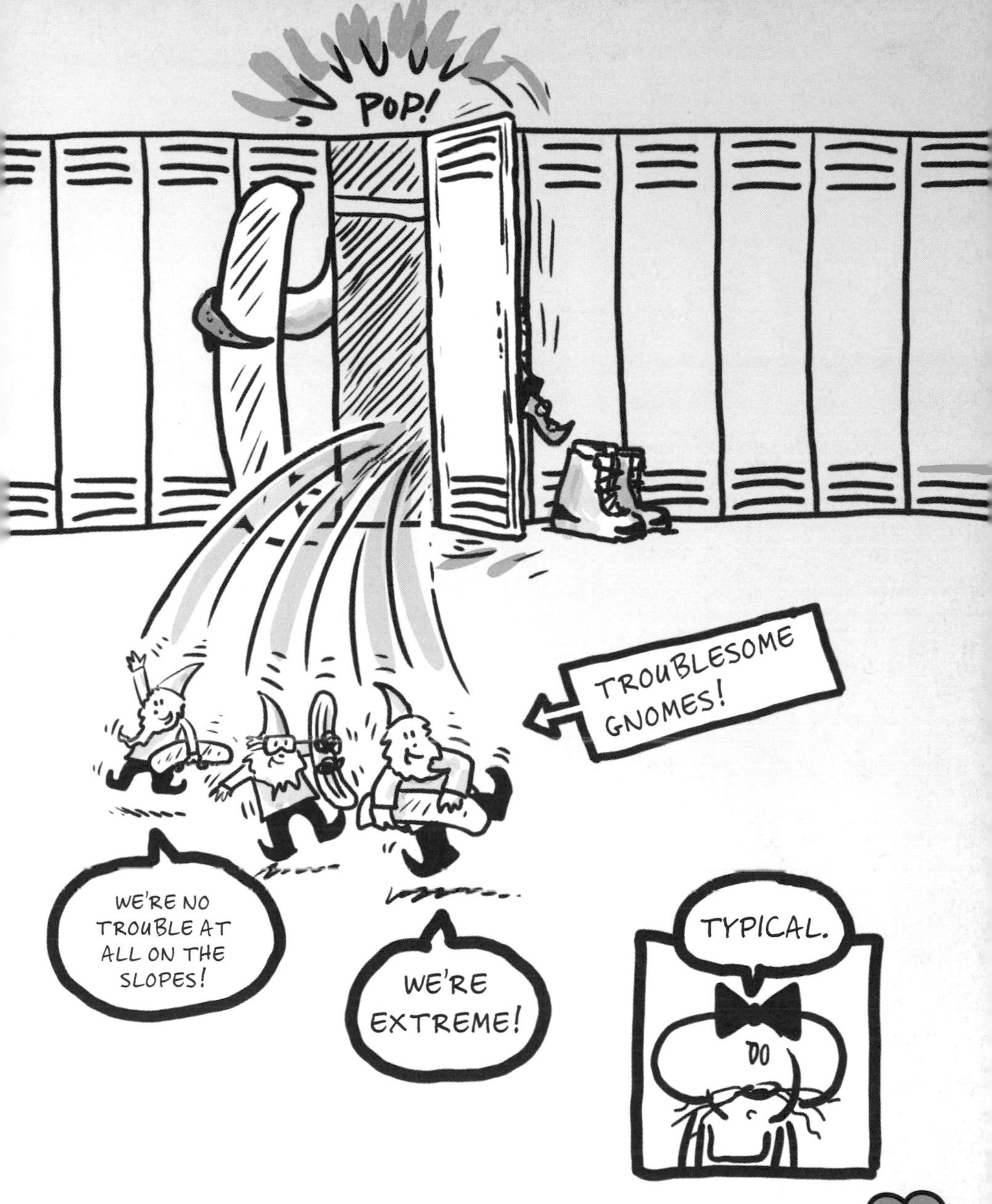
POP!
TROUBLESOME GNOMES!
WE'RE NO TROUBLE AT ALL ON THE SLOPES!
WE'RE EXTREME!
TYPICAL.

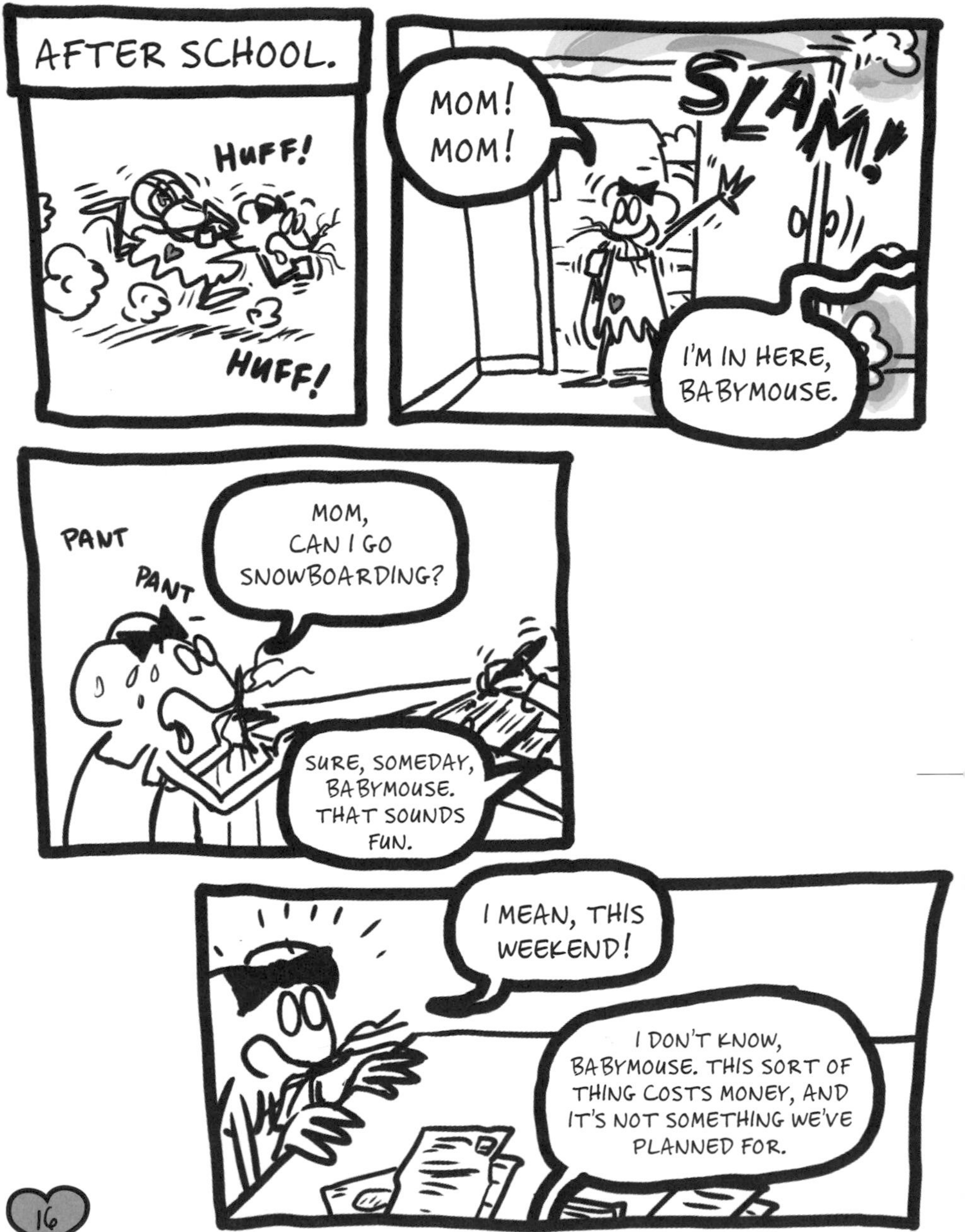
AFTER SCHOOL.
HUFF!
HUFF!
MOM! MOM!
SLAM!
I'M IN HERE, BABYMOUSE.
PANT
PANT
MOM, CAN I GO SNOWBOARDING?
SURE, SOMEDAY, BABYMOUSE. THAT SOUNDS FUN.
I MEAN, THIS WEEKEND!
I DON'T KNOW, BABYMOUSE. THIS SORT OF THING COSTS MONEY, AND IT'S NOT SOMETHING WE'VE PLANNED FOR.

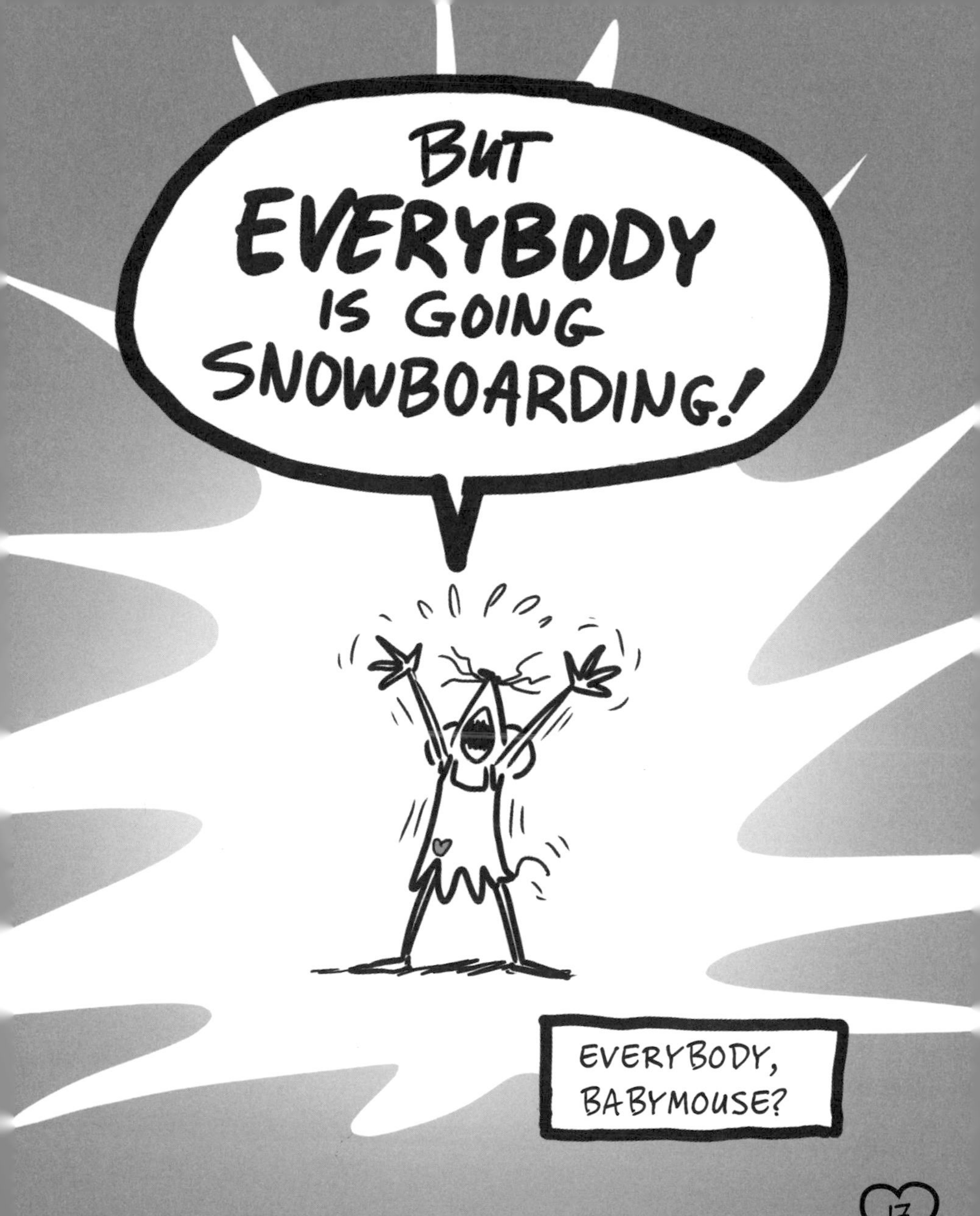
BUT EVERYBODY IS GOING SNOWBOARDING!
EVERYBODY, BABYMOUSE?

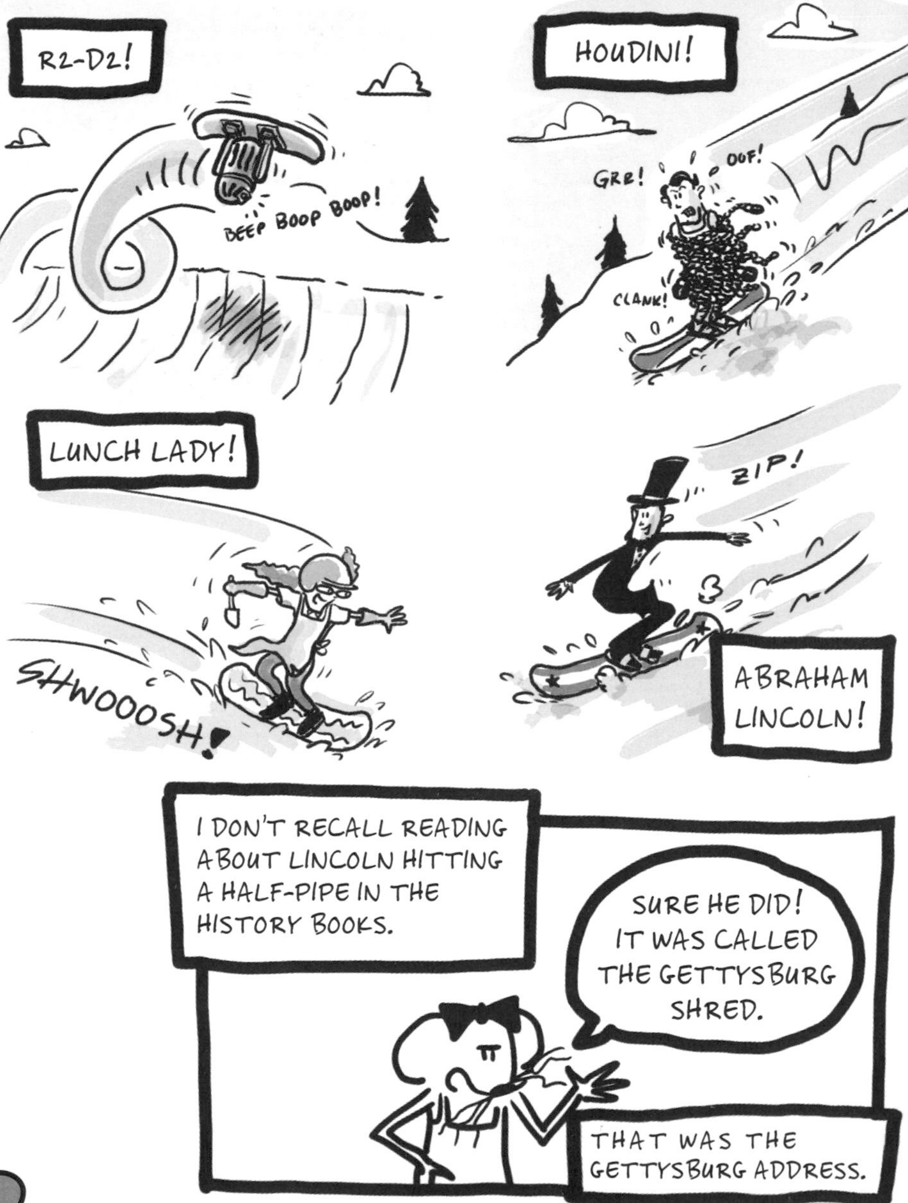
R2-D2!
BEEP BOOP BOOP!
HOUDINI!
GRR!
OOF!
CLANK!
LUNCH LADY!
SHWOOOSH!
ZIP!
ABRAHAM LINCOLN!
I DON'T RECALL READING ABOUT LINCOLN HITTING A HALF-PIPE IN THE HISTORY BOOKS.
SURE HE DID! IT WAS CALLED THE GETTYSBURG SHRED.
THAT WAS THE GETTYSBURG ADDRESS.

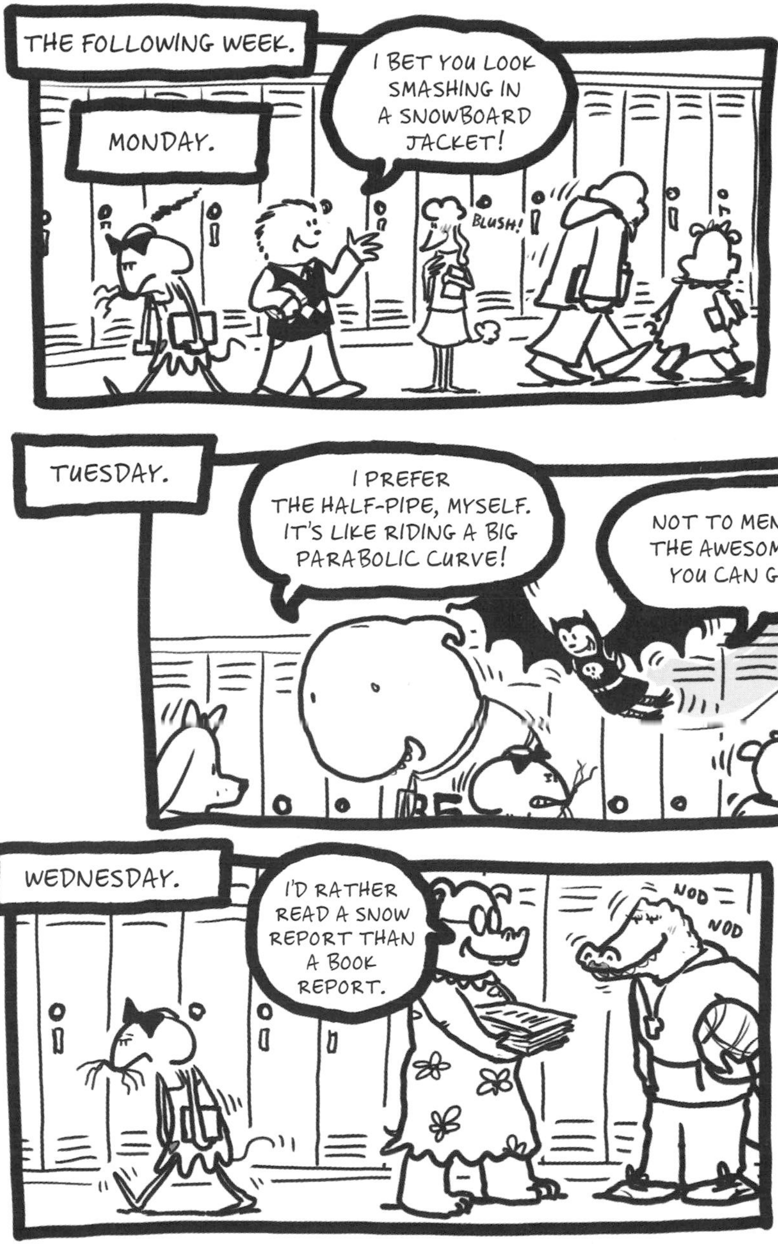
THE FOLLOWING WEEK.
MONDAY.
I BET YOU LOOK SMASHING IN A SNOWBOARD JACKET!
BLUSH!
TUESDAY.
I PREFER THE HALF-PIPE, MYSELF. IT'S LIKE RIDING A BIG PARABOLIC CURVE!
NOT TO MENTION THE AWESOME AIR YOU CAN GET!
WEDNESDAY.
I'D RATHER READ A SNOW REPORT THAN A BOOK REPORT.
NOD
NOD

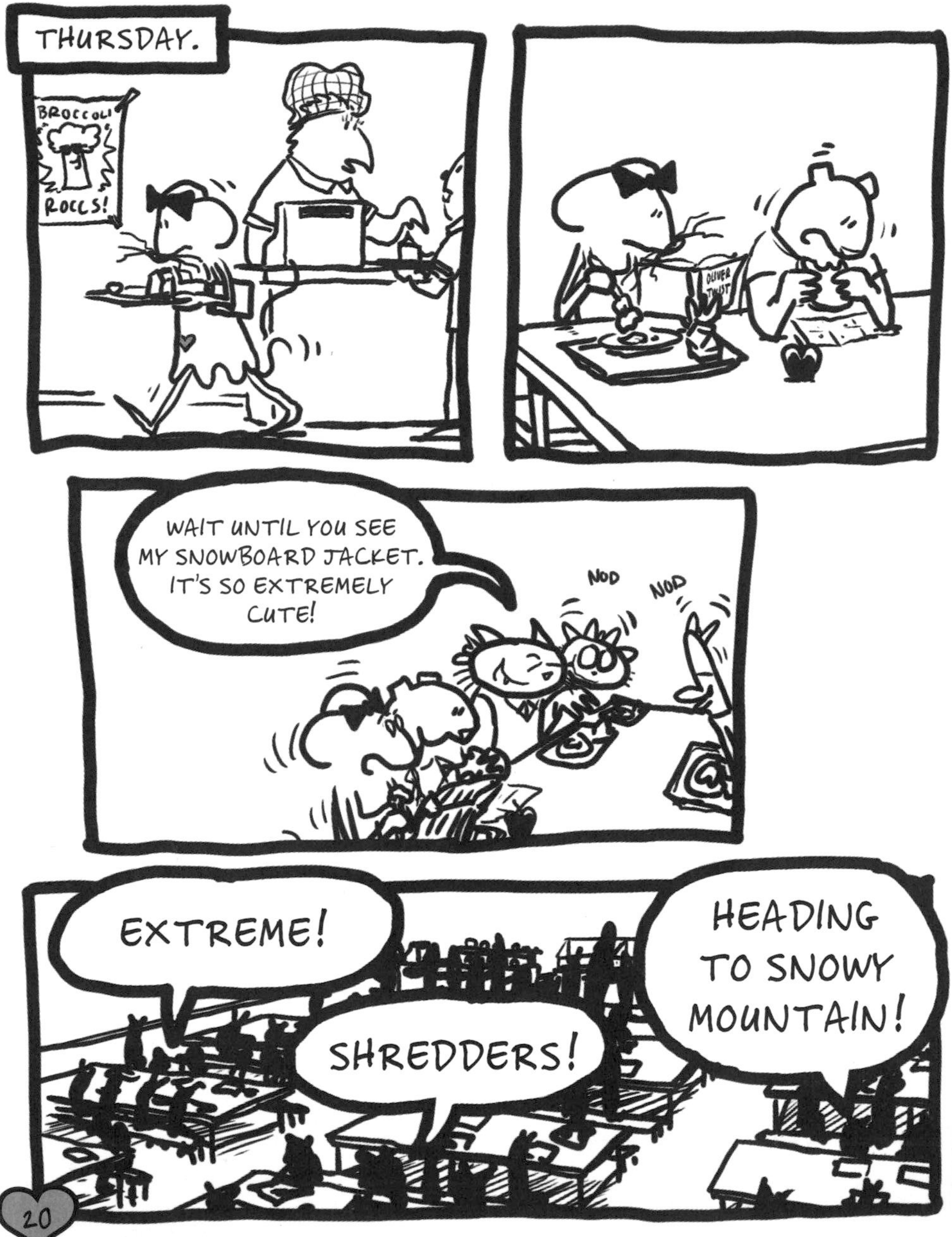
THURSDAY.
BROCCOLI ROCKS!
OLIVER TWIST
WAIT UNTIL YOU SEE MY SNOWBOARD JACKET. IT'S SO EXTREMELY CUTE!
NOD
NOD
EXTREME!
SHREDDERS!
HEADING TO SNOWY MOUNTAIN!

XTREME! GET YOUR BOARD WAXED! DU
BLACK DIAMOND ALL THE WAY! GONNA B
SWEET, SWEET, SWEET! SHREDDERS!!!
OPE CONDITIONS WILL BE EPIC! I CAN'T
VAIT TO HIT THE RAILS, DUDE! NEED TO
OWDER! I'M GOOFY! WE'RE TOTALLY GO
HRED THE BACKSIDE BEFORE WE HIT T
ALF-PIPE. SHE'S SUCH AN AIRDOG! TOT
XTREME! SHOULD HAVE RUN THE CHUT
AN! THAT WAS AN OLLIE YOU COULD PU
HE BOOKS! SHAVE THAT SIDE! THERE'S
ONNA BE FRESHIES! DID YOU SEE HER 5
CTWIST? THAT WAS SO EXTR !! TE
OU'RE READY WE'LL GET T S
AXED UP AND HIT IT AT FIR !

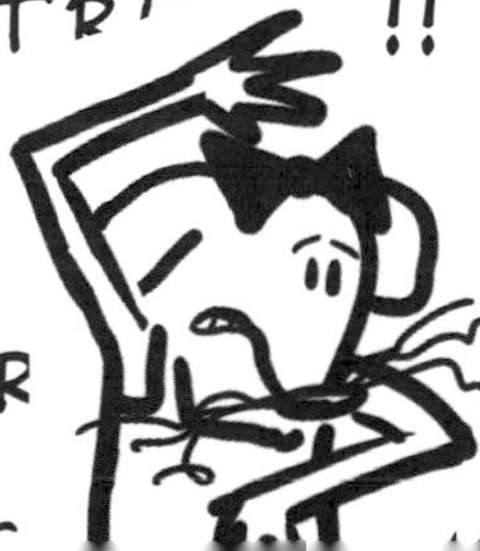

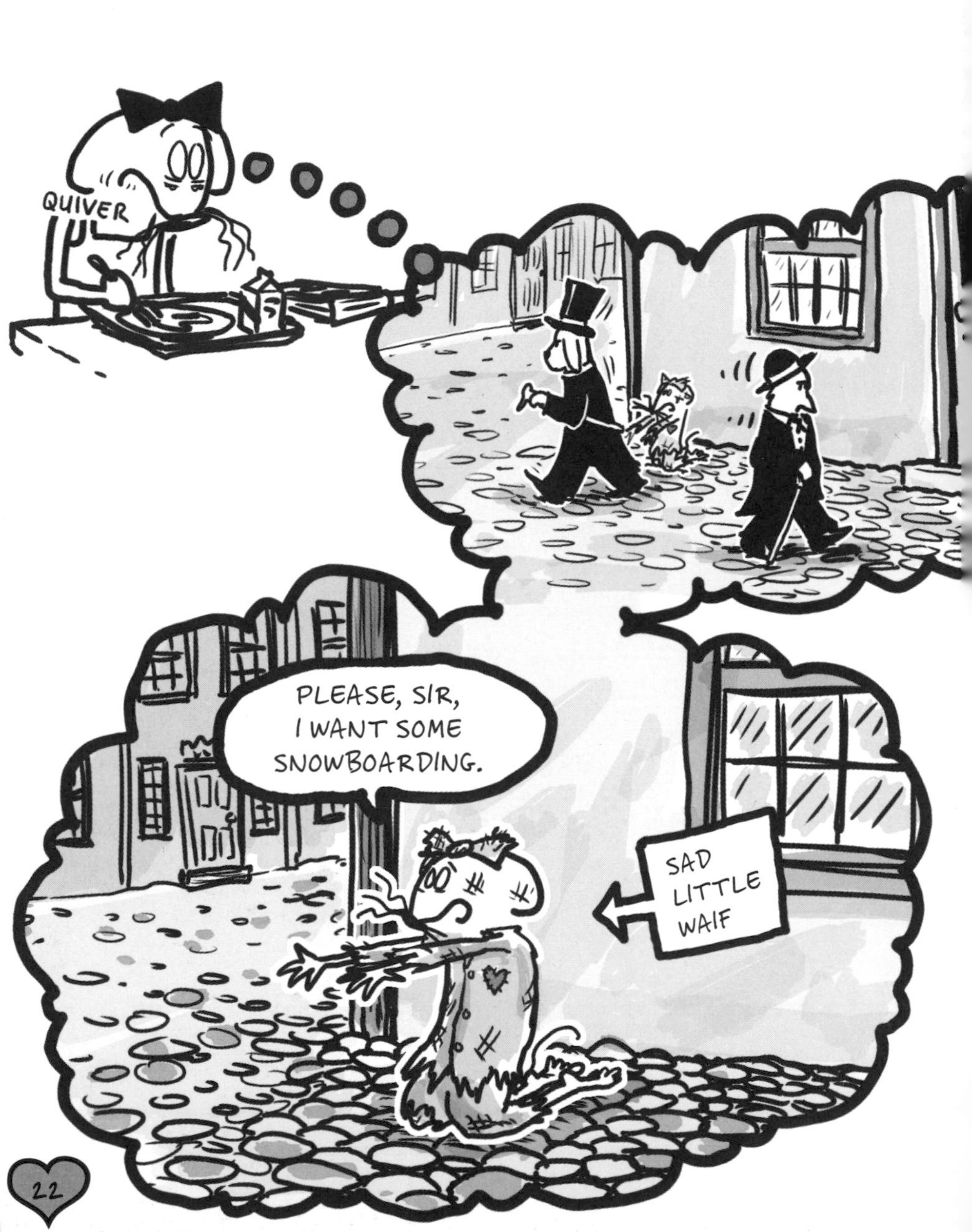
QUIVER
PLEASE, SIR, I WANT SOME SNOWBOARDING.
SAD LITTLE WAIF

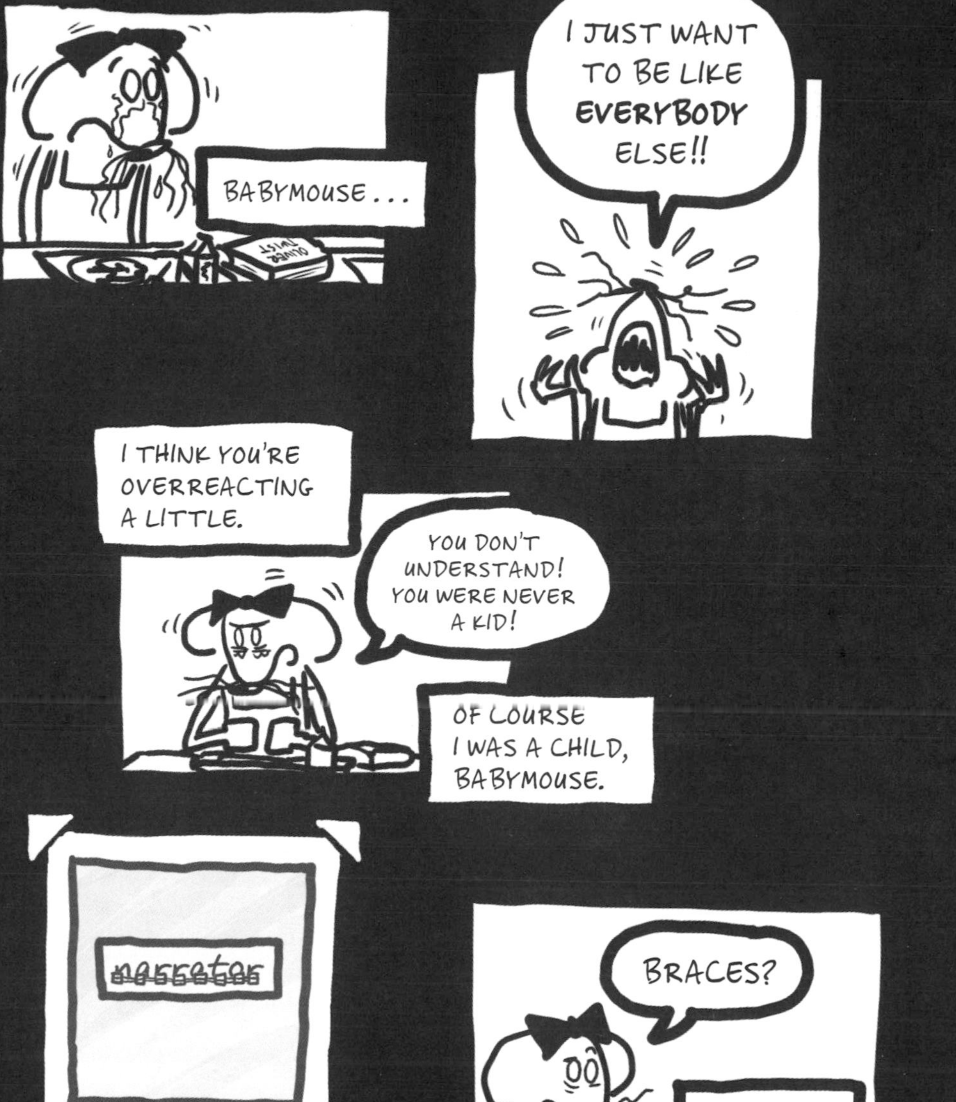
BABYMOUSE . . .
OLIVER TWIST
I JUST WANT TO BE LIKE **EVERYBODY** ELSE!!
I THINK YOU'RE OVERREACTING A LITTLE.
YOU DON'T UNDERSTAND! YOU WERE NEVER A KID!
OF COURSE I WAS A CHILD, BABYMOUSE.
~~narrator~~
"Narrator" - 11 years old
BRACES?
I HAD AN OVERBITE.

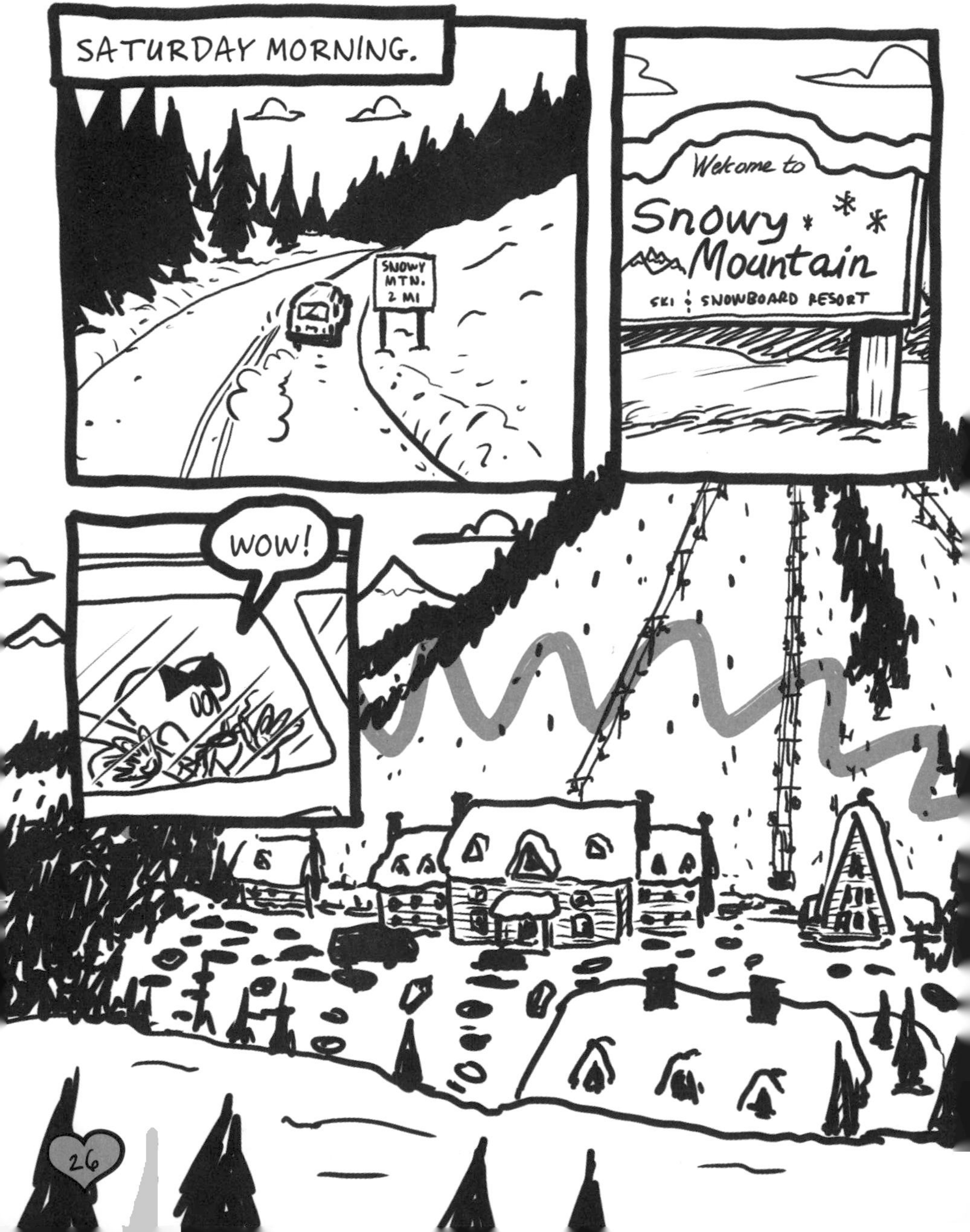
SATURDAY MORNING.
SNOWY MTN. 2 MI
Welcome to
Snowy Mountain
SKI & SNOWBOARD RESORT
WOW!

27

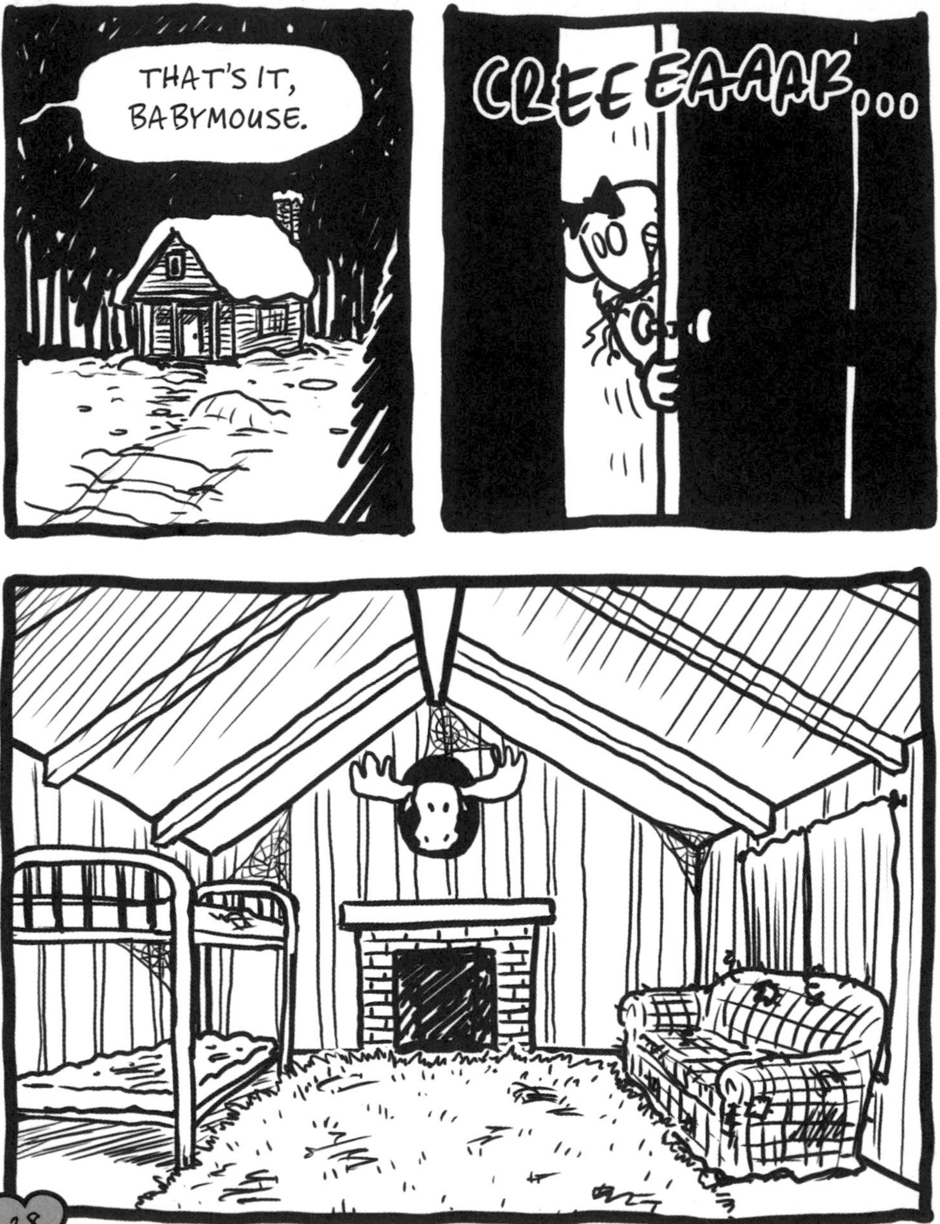
THAT'S IT, BABYMOUSE.
CREEEEAAAK...

WHERE'S THE HOT TUB?

I THINK YOU'LL BE LUCKY TO HAVE HOT WATER, BABYMOUSE.

DRIP

DRIP

TYPICAL.

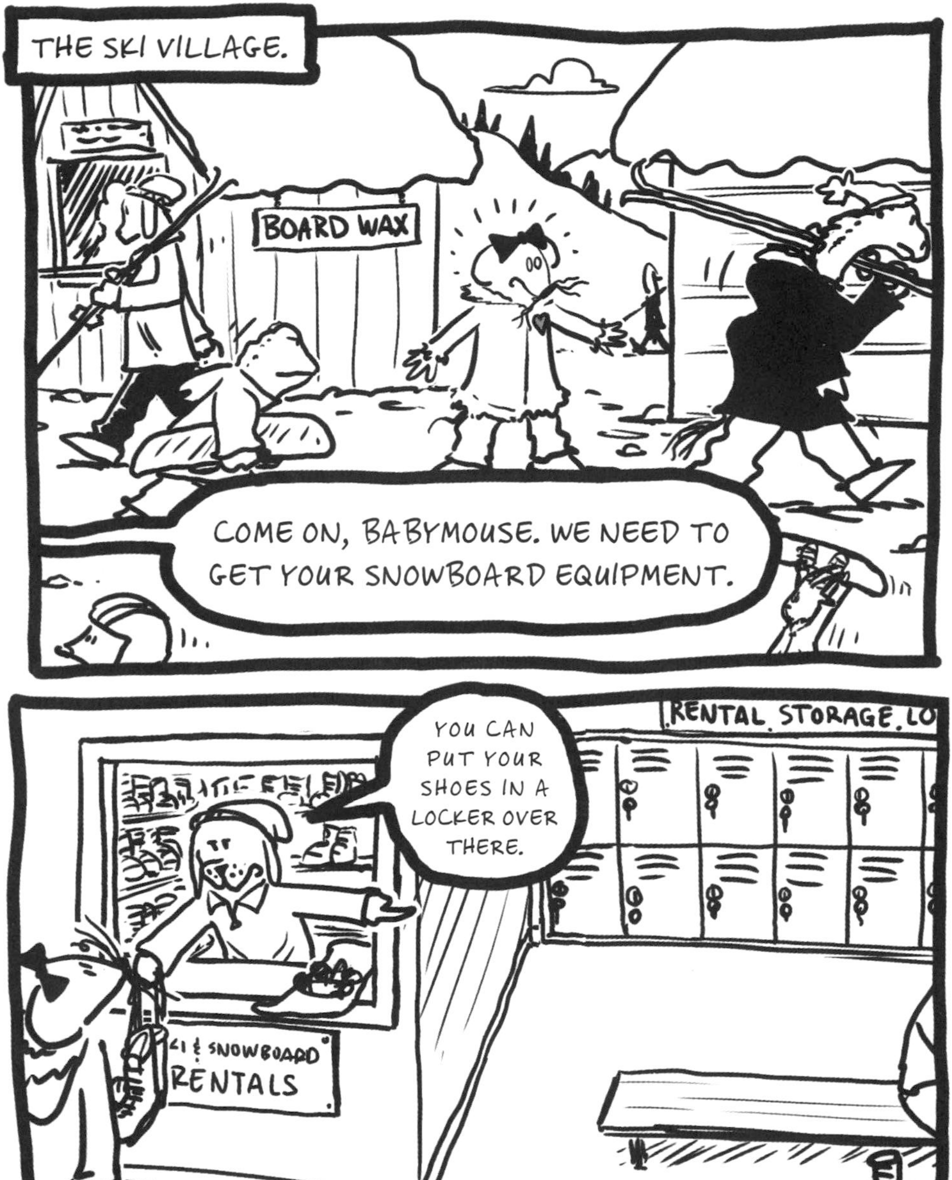
THE SKI VILLAGE.
BOARD WAX
COME ON, BABYMOUSE. WE NEED TO GET YOUR SNOWBOARD EQUIPMENT.
RENTAL STORAGE LO
YOU CAN PUT YOUR SHOES IN A LOCKER OVER THERE.
SNOWBOARD RENTALS

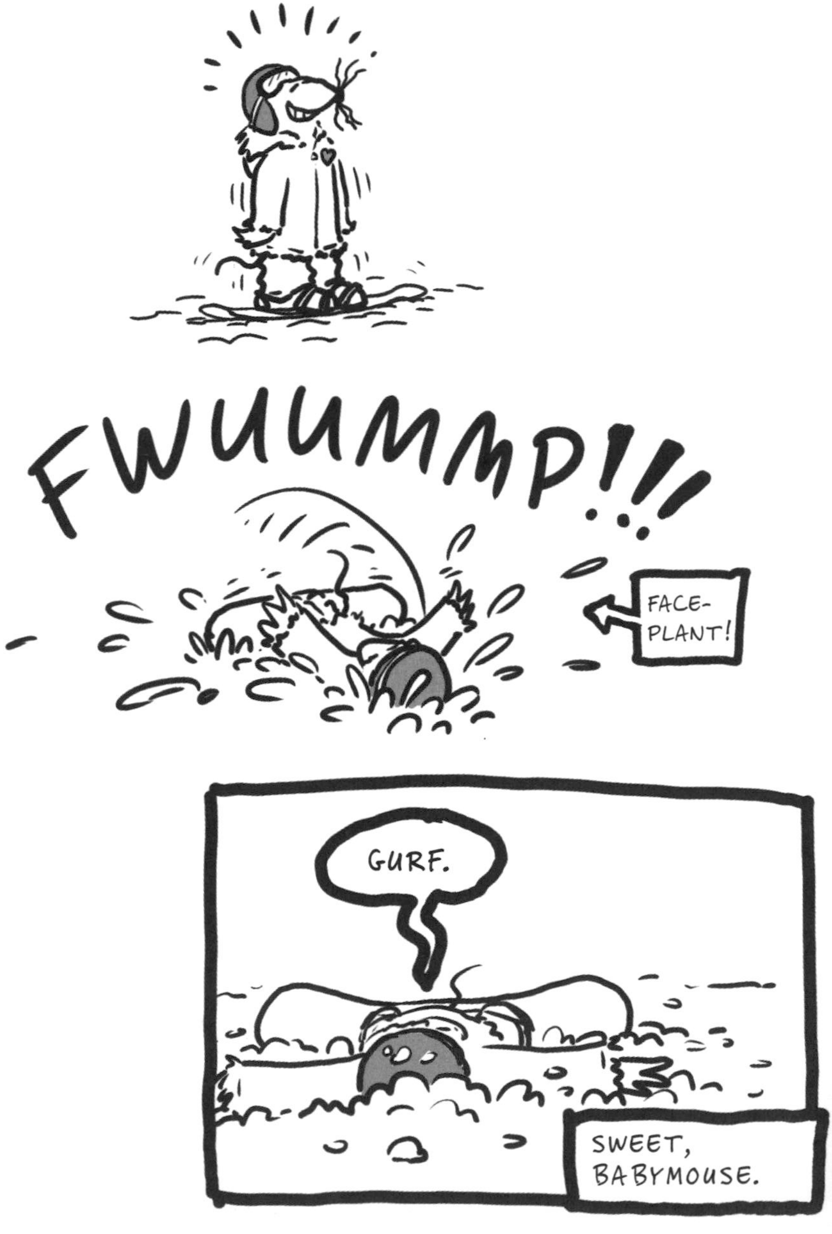
FWUUMMP!!!
FACE-PLANT!
GURF.
SWEET, BABYMOUSE.

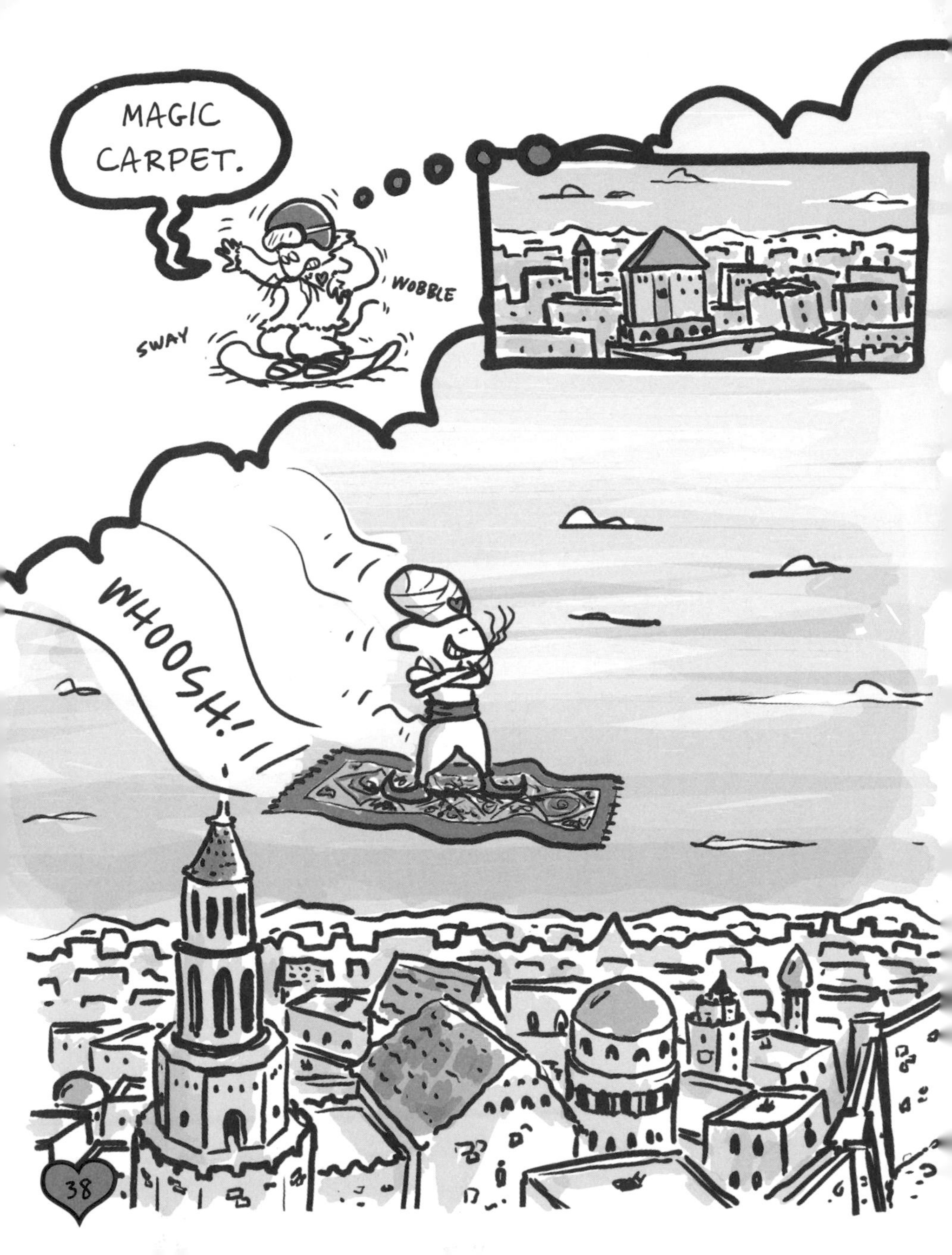
MAGIC CARPET.
WOBBLE
SWAY
WHOOSH!

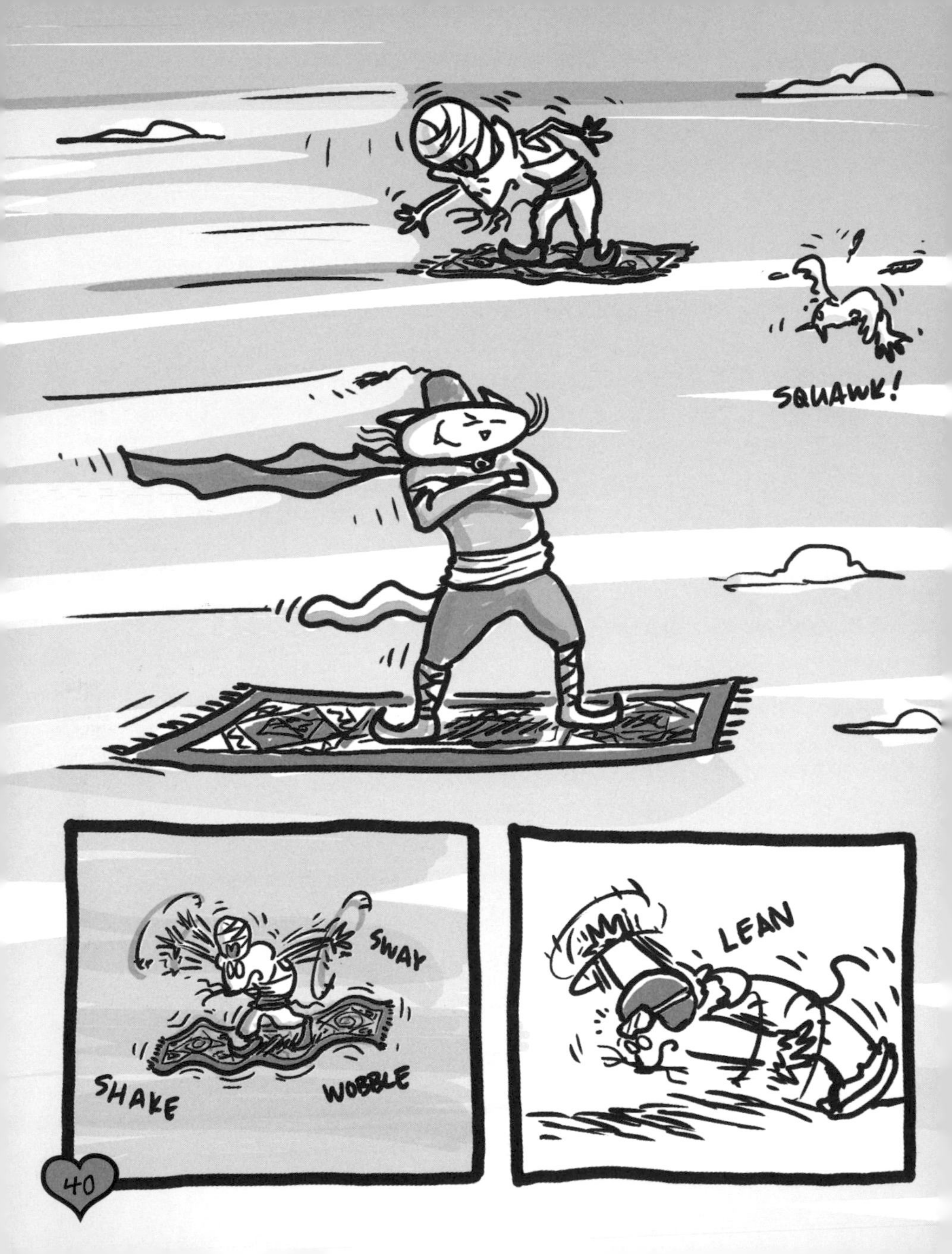
SQUAWK!
SWAY
SHAKE
WOBBLE
LEAN

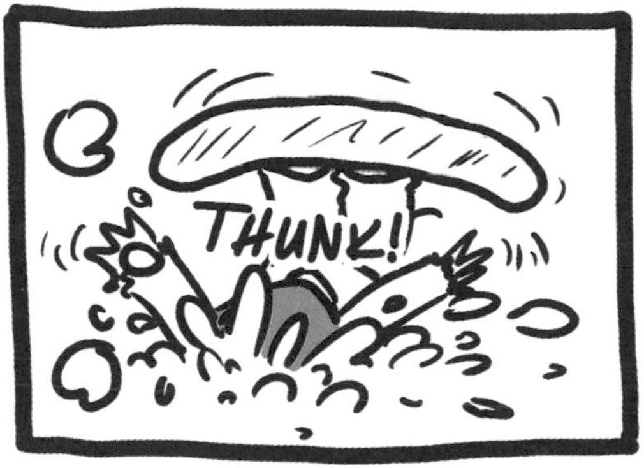
THUNK!

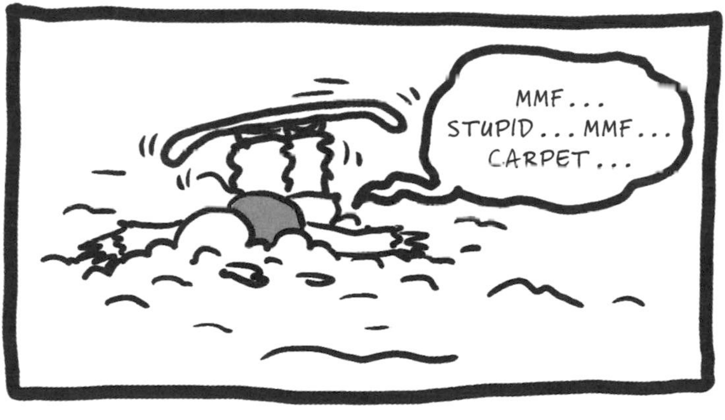
MMF... STUPID... MMF... CARPET...

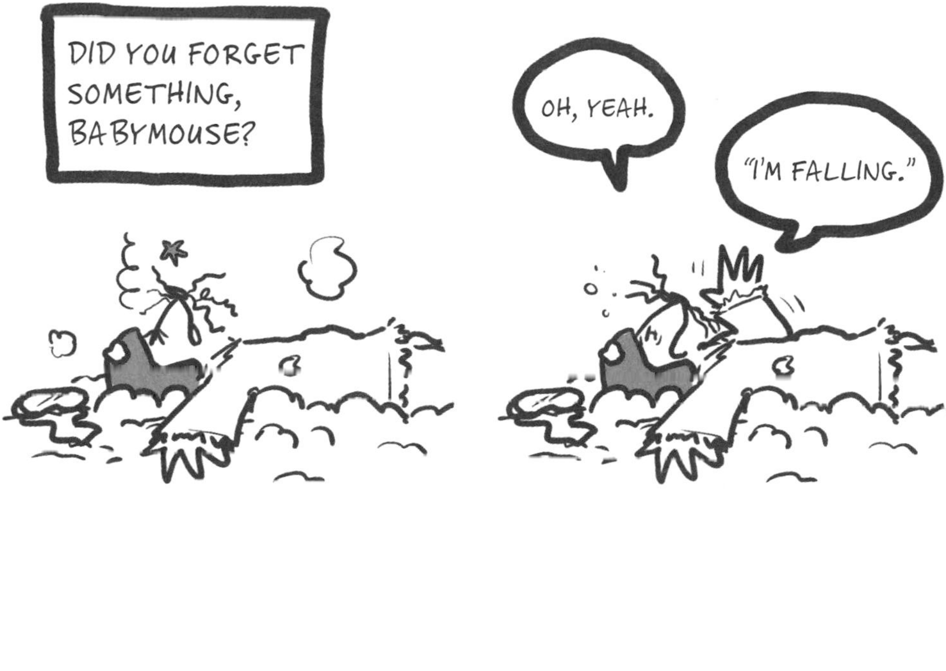
DID YOU FORGET SOMETHING, BABYMOUSE?
OH, YEAH.
"I'M FALLING."

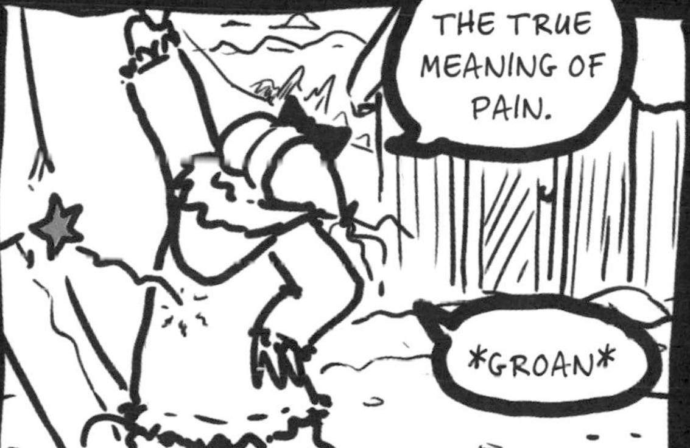
THE TRUE MEANING OF PAIN.
GROAN

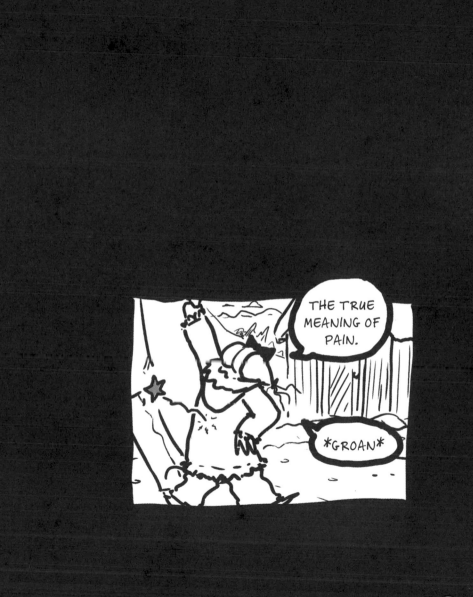

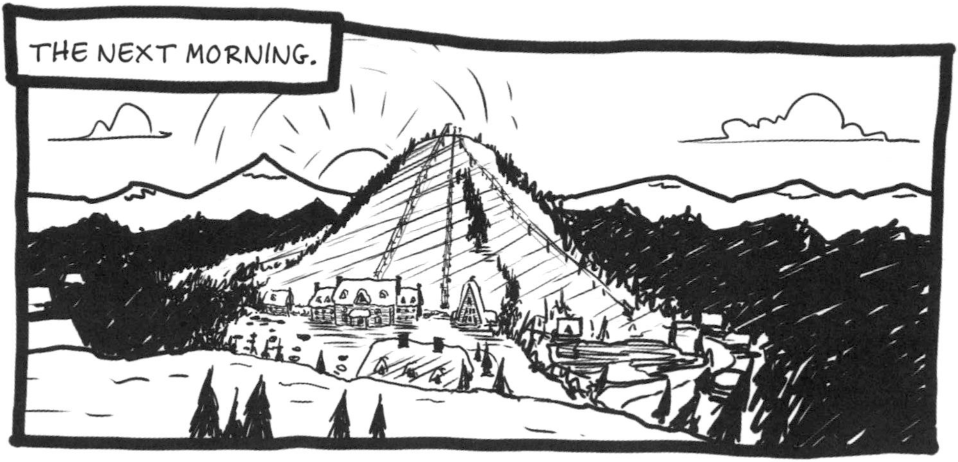
THE NEXT MORNING.

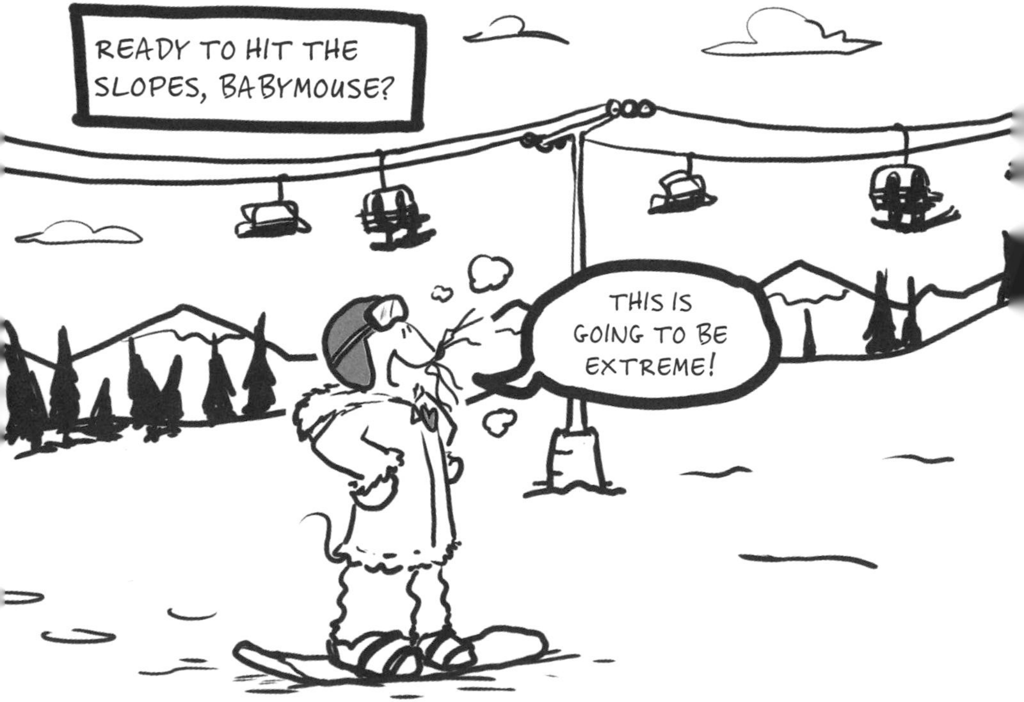
READY TO HIT THE SLOPES, BABYMOUSE?
THIS IS GOING TO BE EXTREME!

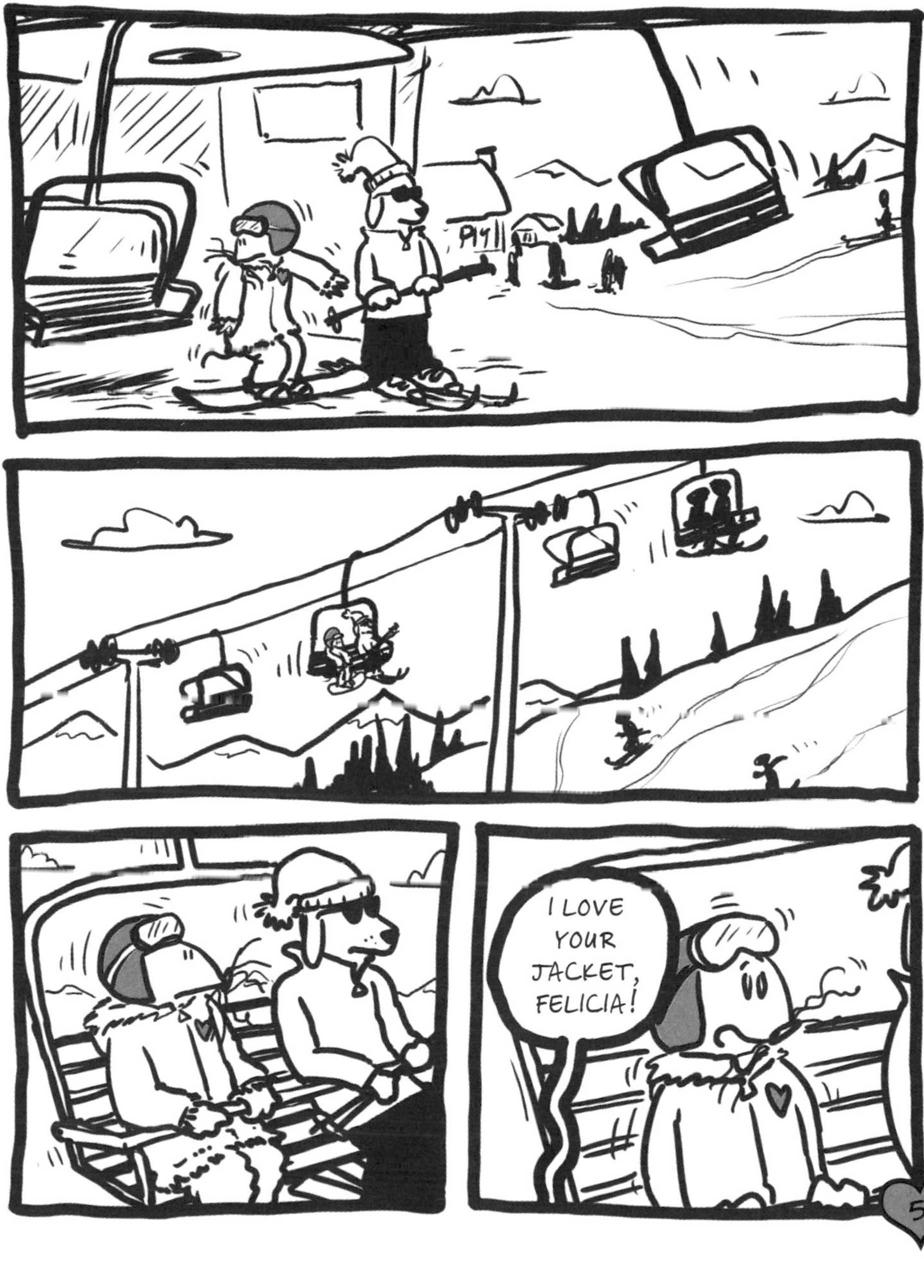
I LOVE YOUR JACKET, FELICIA!

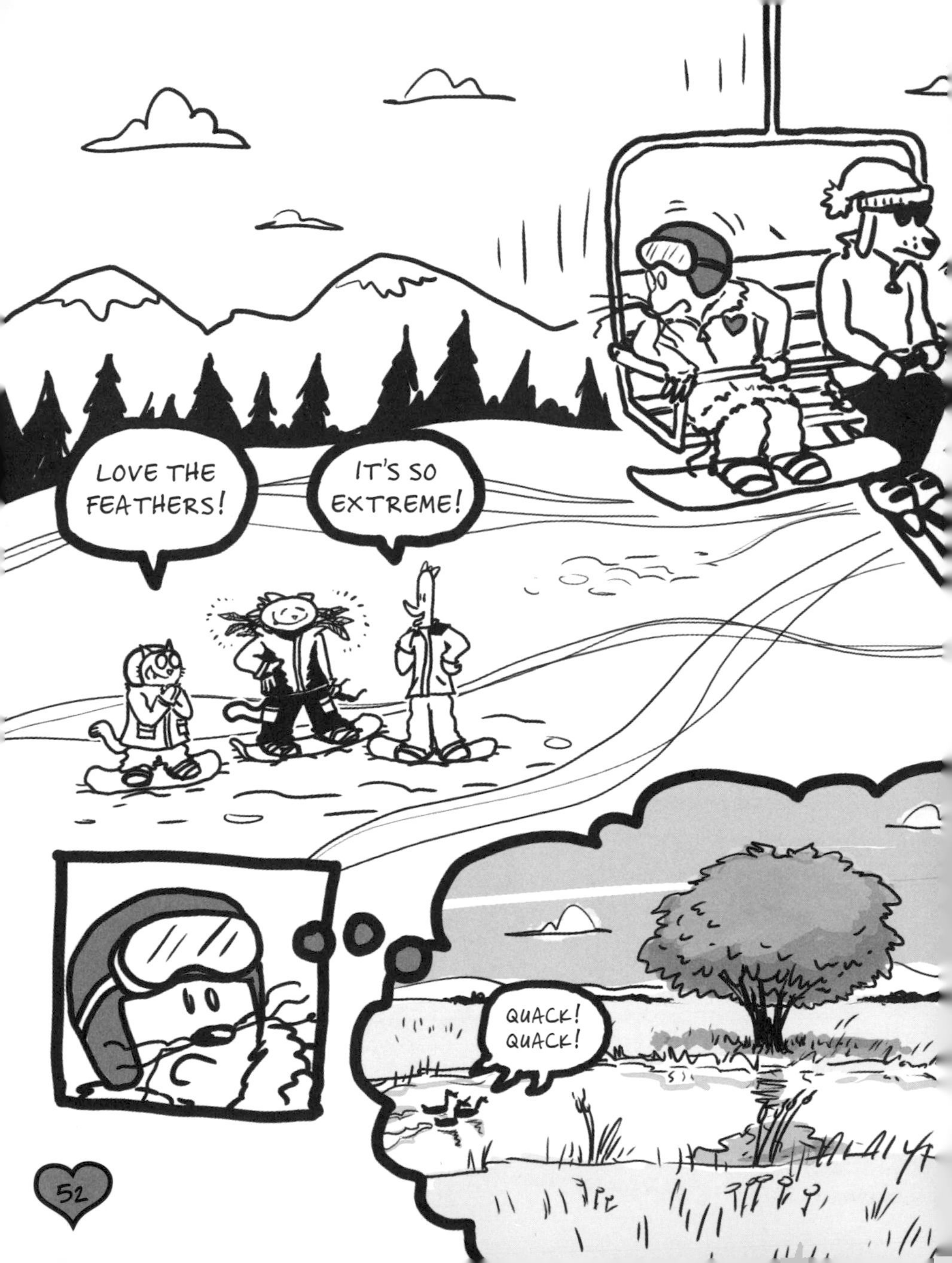
LOVE THE FEATHERS!
IT'S SO EXTREME!
QUACK! QUACK!

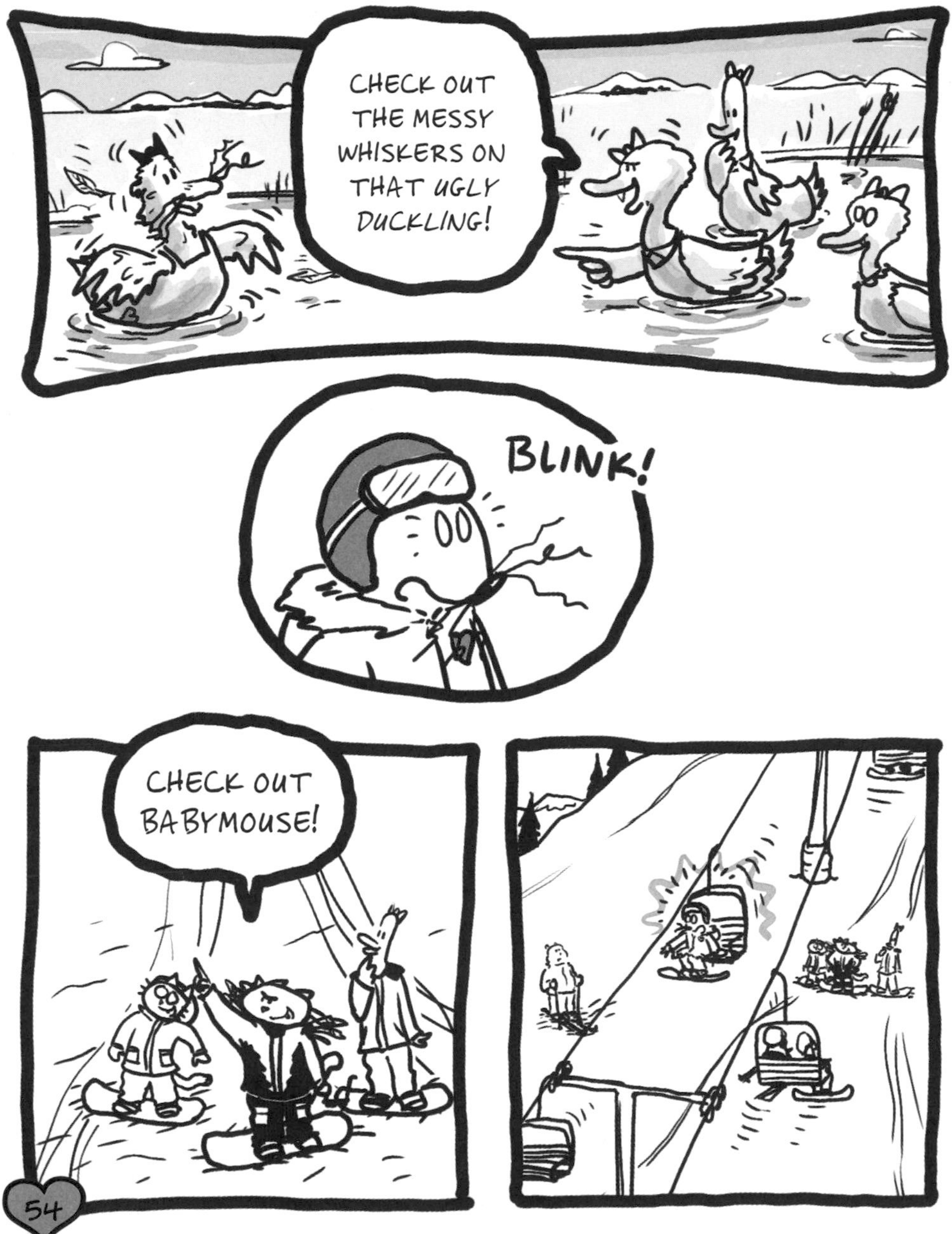
CHECK OUT THE MESSY WHISKERS ON THAT UGLY DUCKLING!
BLINK!
CHECK OUT BABYMOUSE!

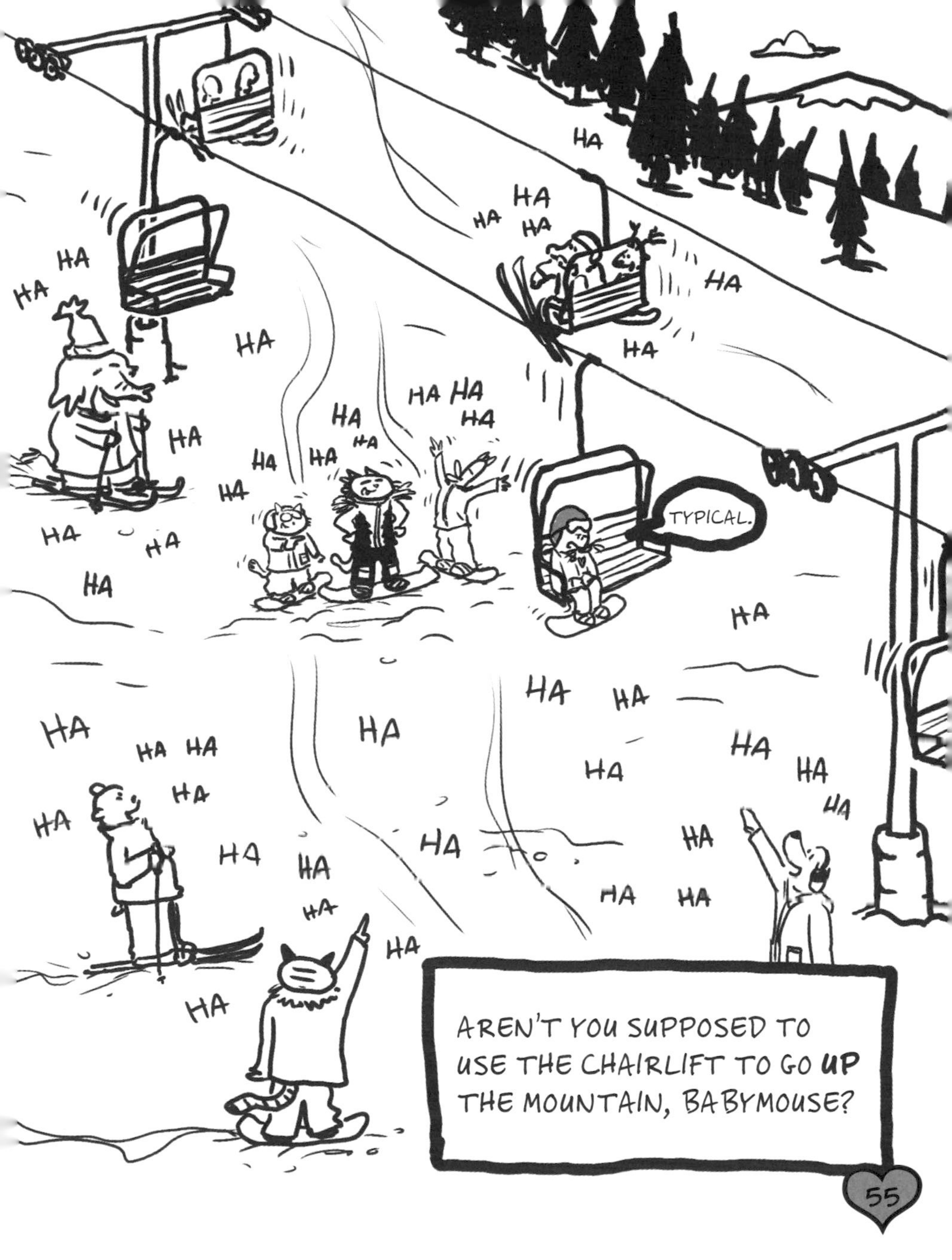
HA
HA HA
HA
HA HA
HA
HA
HA
HA HA
HA
HA
HA
HA
HA
HA
HA
TYPICAL.
HA
HA
HA
HA
HA
HA
HA HA
HA
HA
HA
HA
HA
HA
HA
HA HA
HA
HA
HA
AREN'T YOU SUPPOSED TO USE THE CHAIRLIFT TO GO **UP** THE MOUNTAIN, BABYMOUSE?

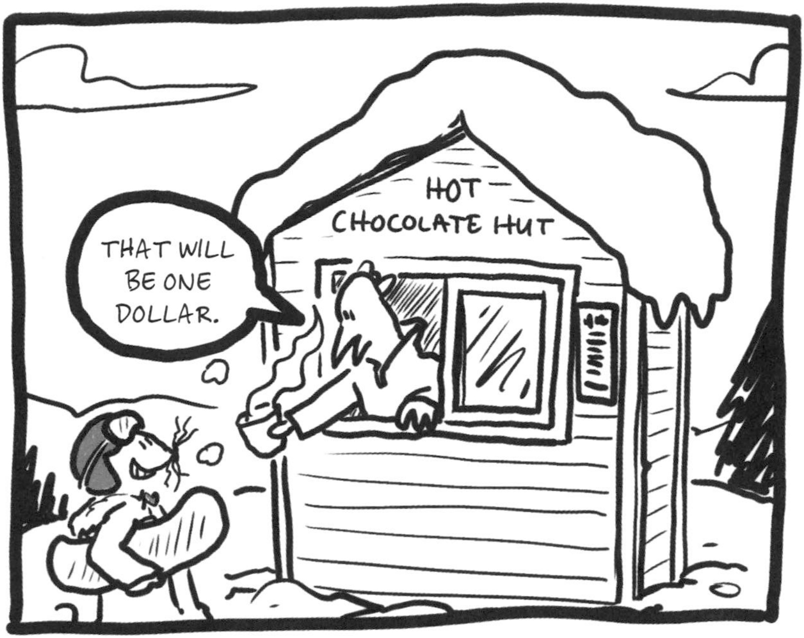
HOT CHOCOLATE HUT
THAT WILL BE ONE DOLLAR.

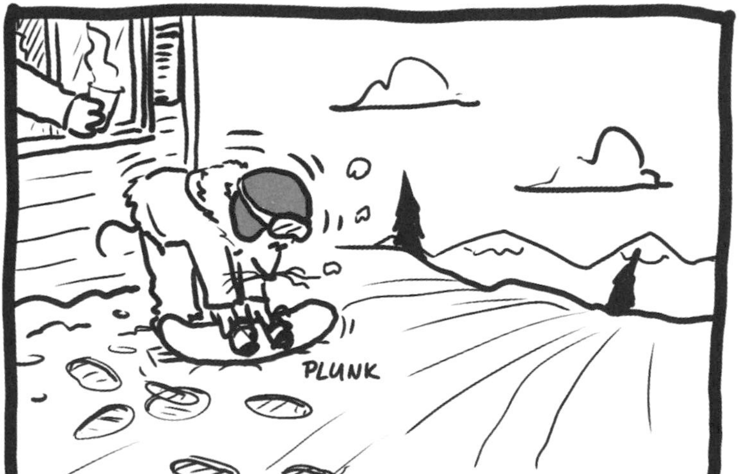
PLUNK

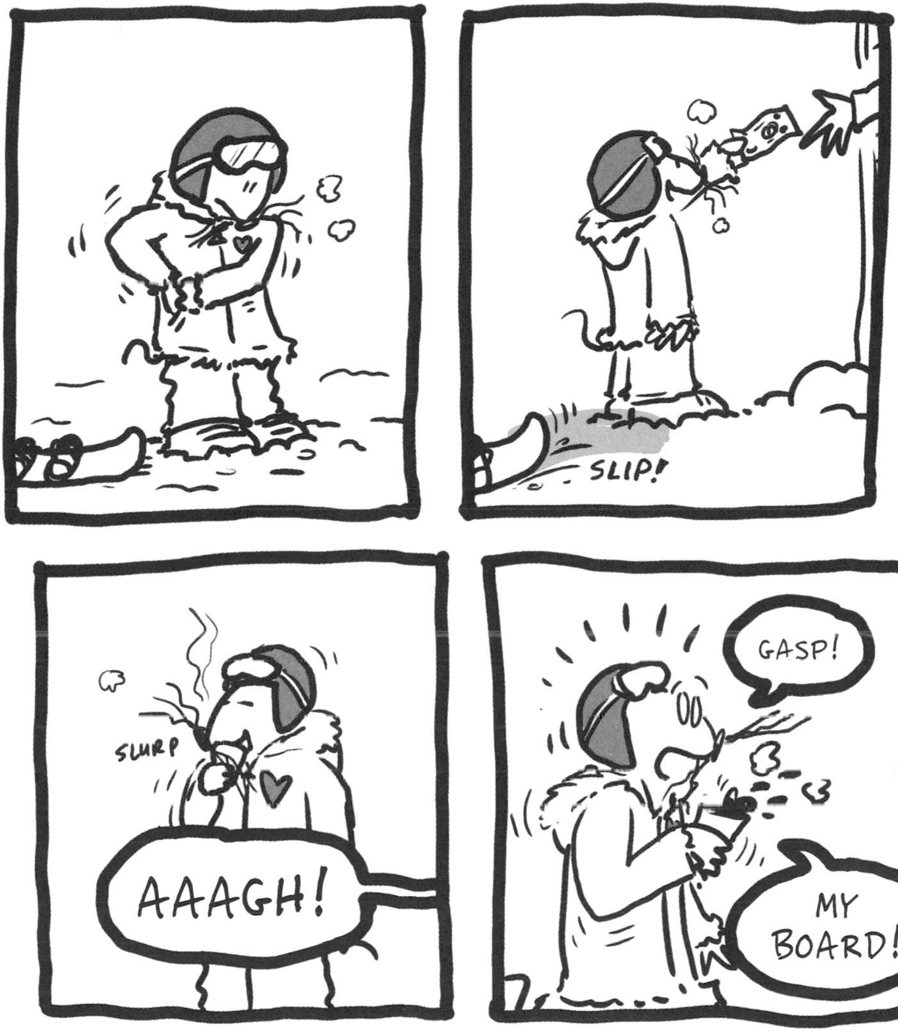
SLIP!
SLURP
AAAGH!
GASP!
MY BOARD!

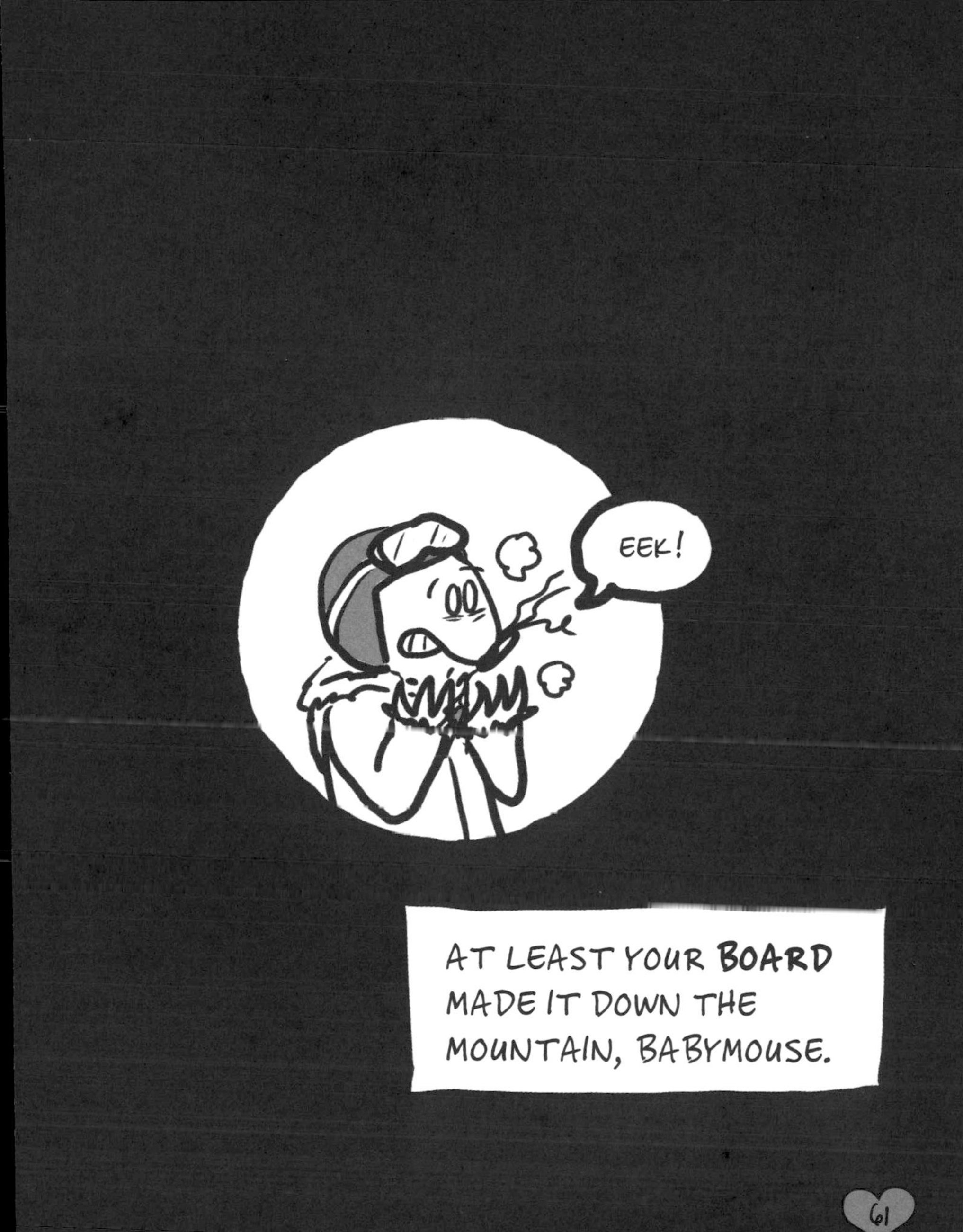
EEK!
AT LEAST YOUR **BOARD** MADE IT DOWN THE MOUNTAIN, BABYMOUSE.

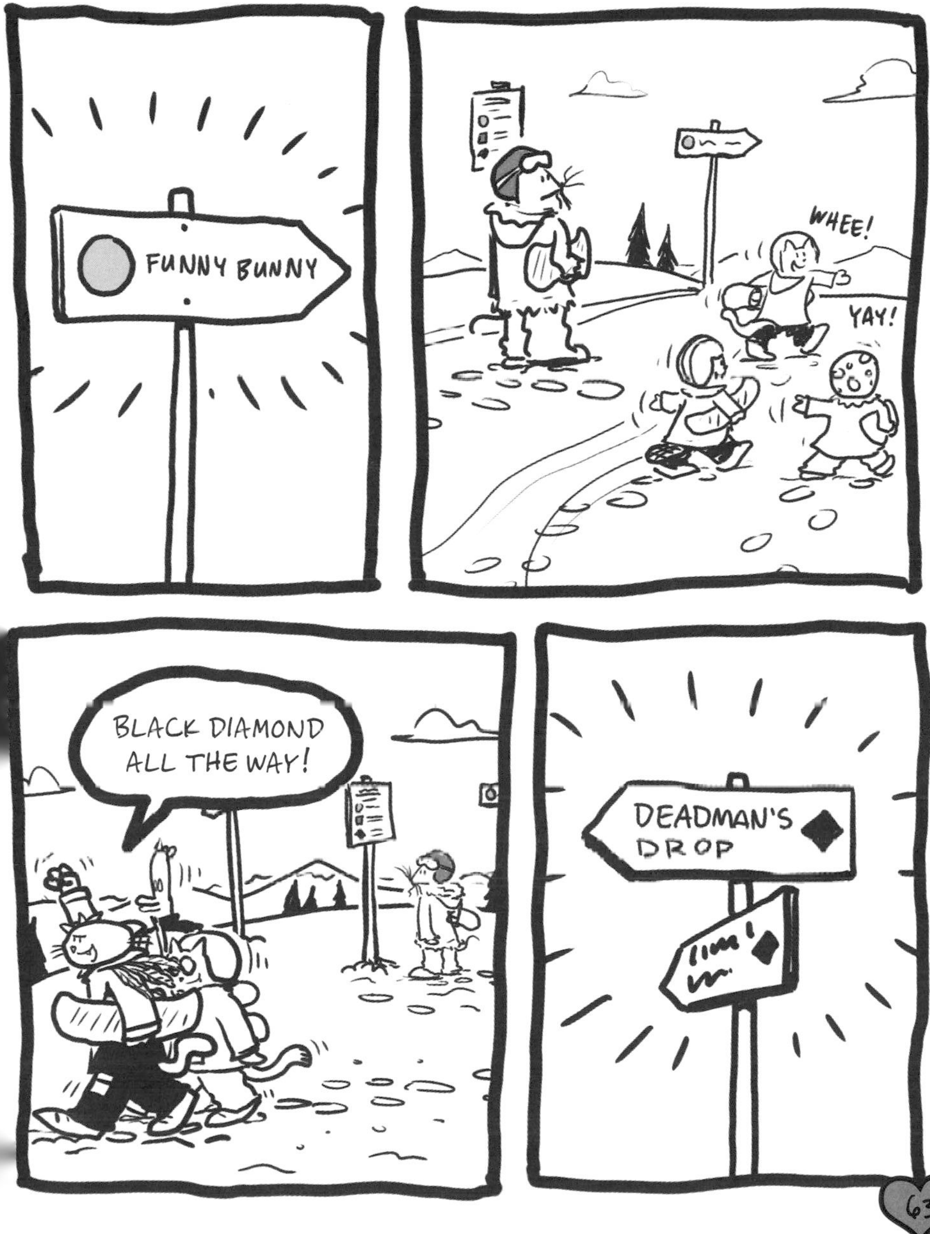
FUNNY BUNNY
WHEE!
YAY!
BLACK DIAMOND ALL THE WAY!
DEADMAN'S DROP

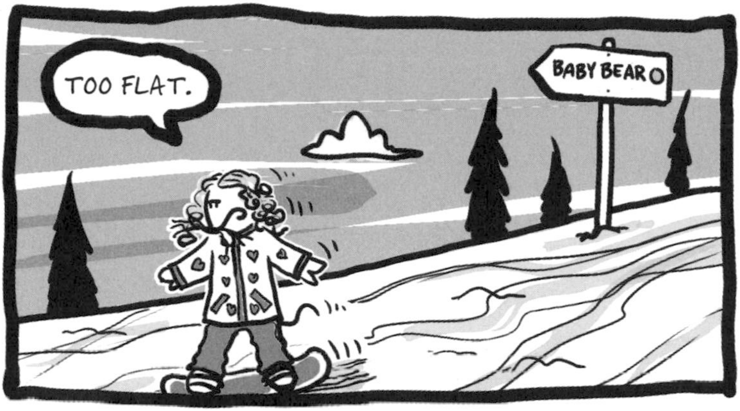
TOO FLAT.
BABY BEAR

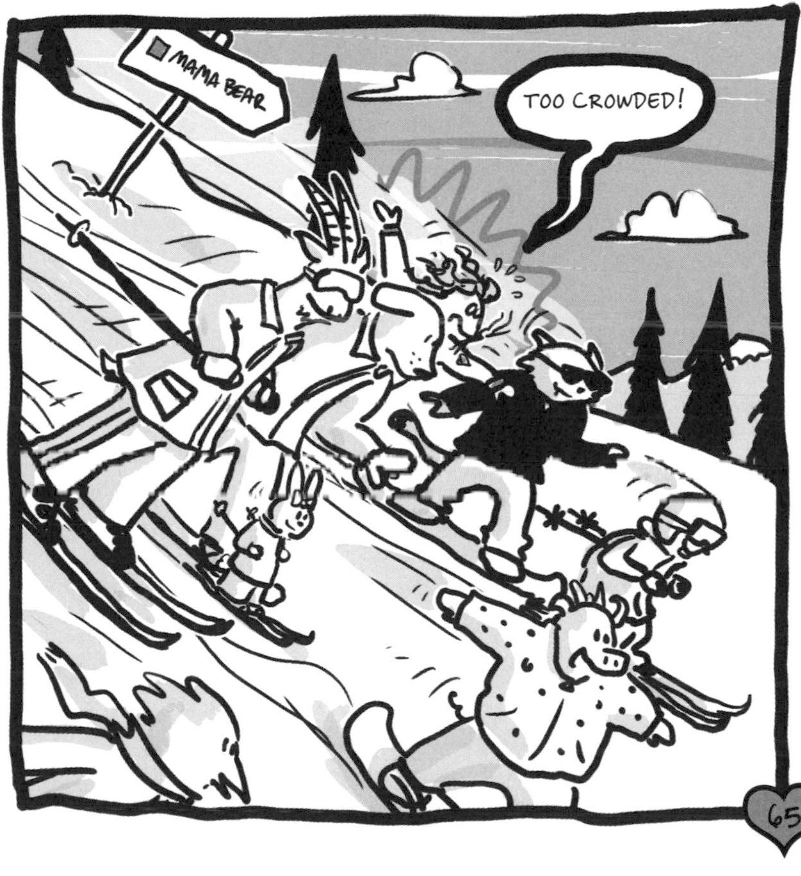
MAMA BEAR
TOO CROWDED!

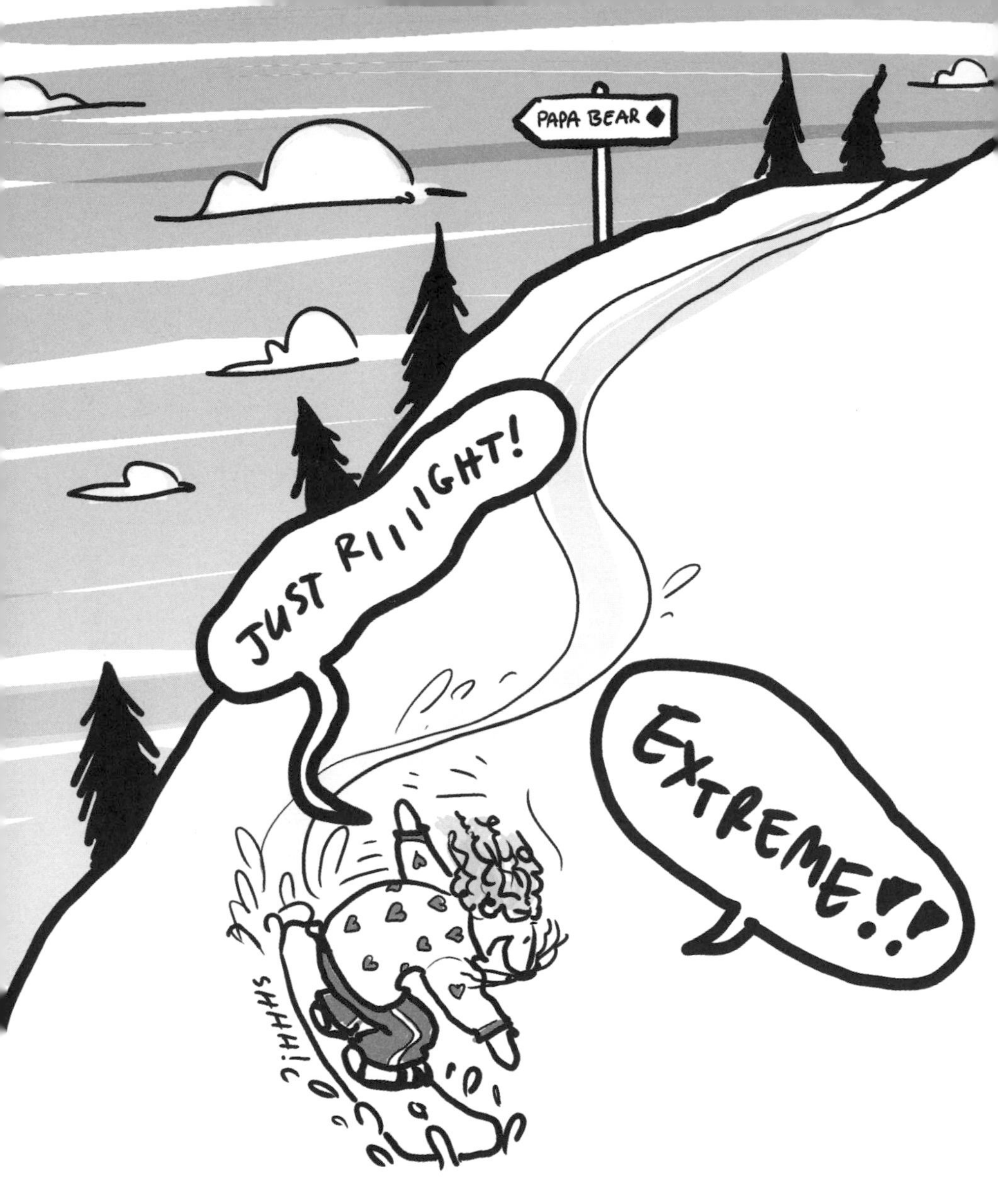
PAPA BEAR
JUST RIIIIGHT!
EXTREME!!
SHHH!

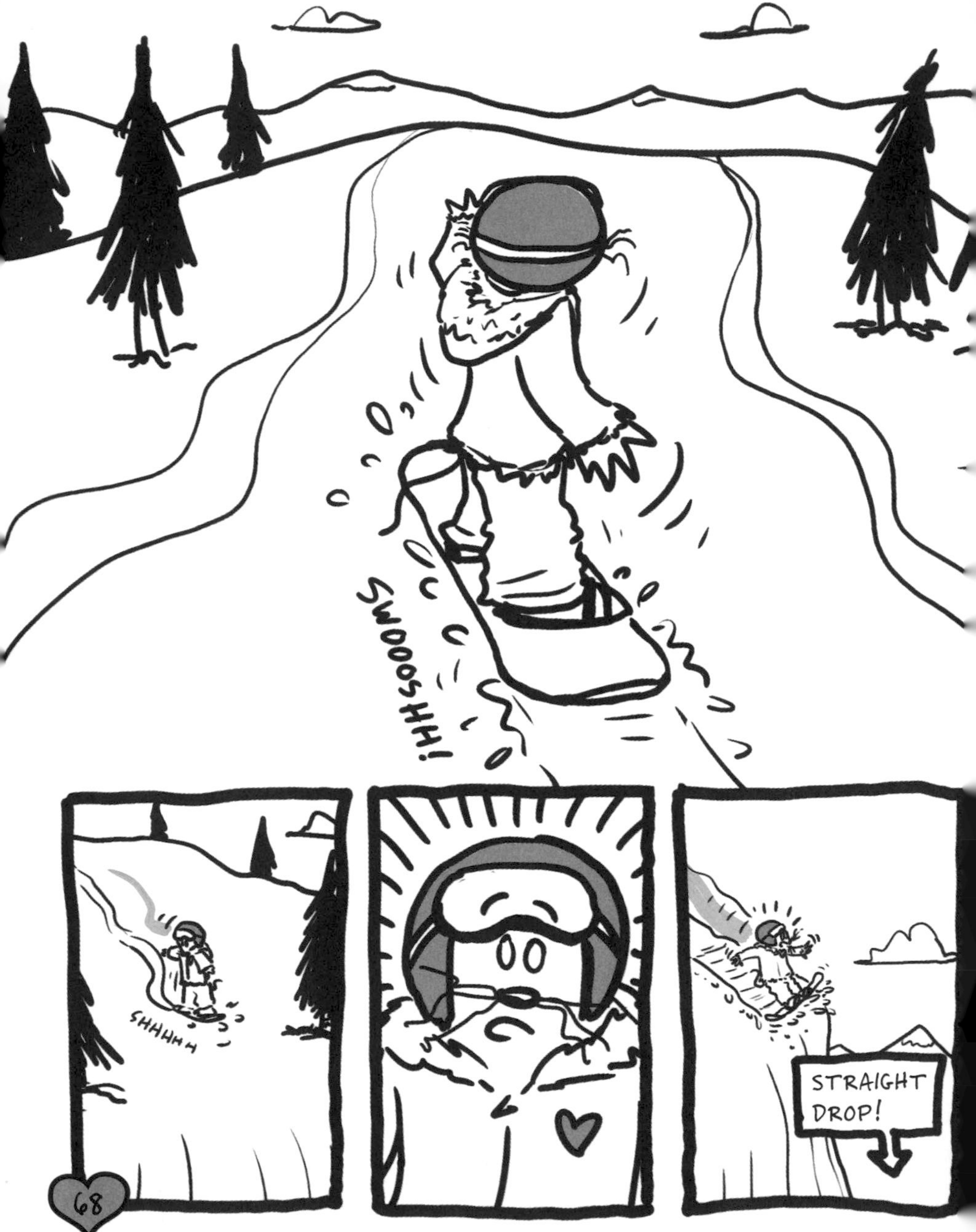
SWOOOSHH!
SHHHHH
STRAIGHT DROP!

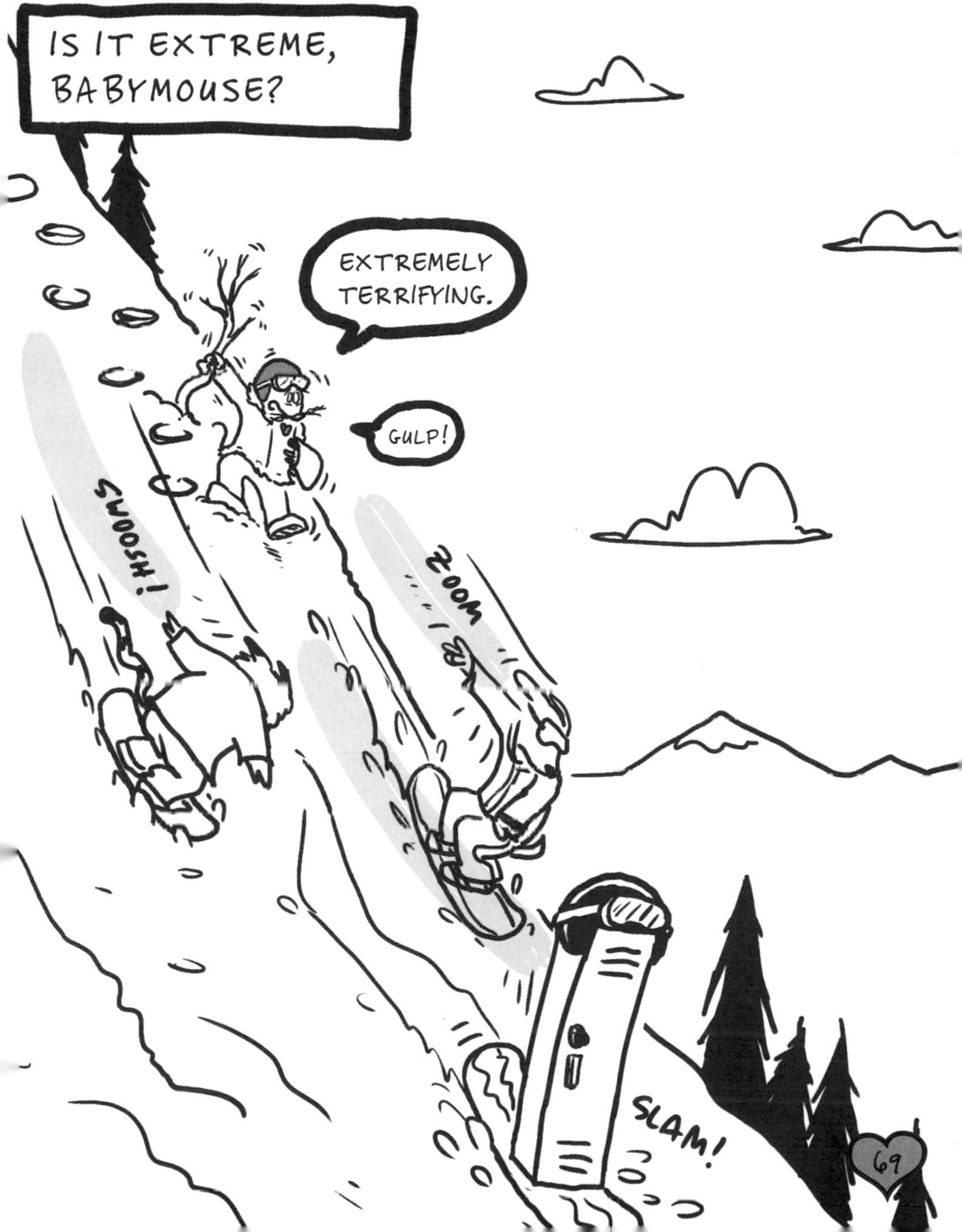
IS IT EXTREME, BABYMOUSE?
EXTREMELY TERRIFYING.
GULP!
SWOOSH!
ZOOM
SLAM!

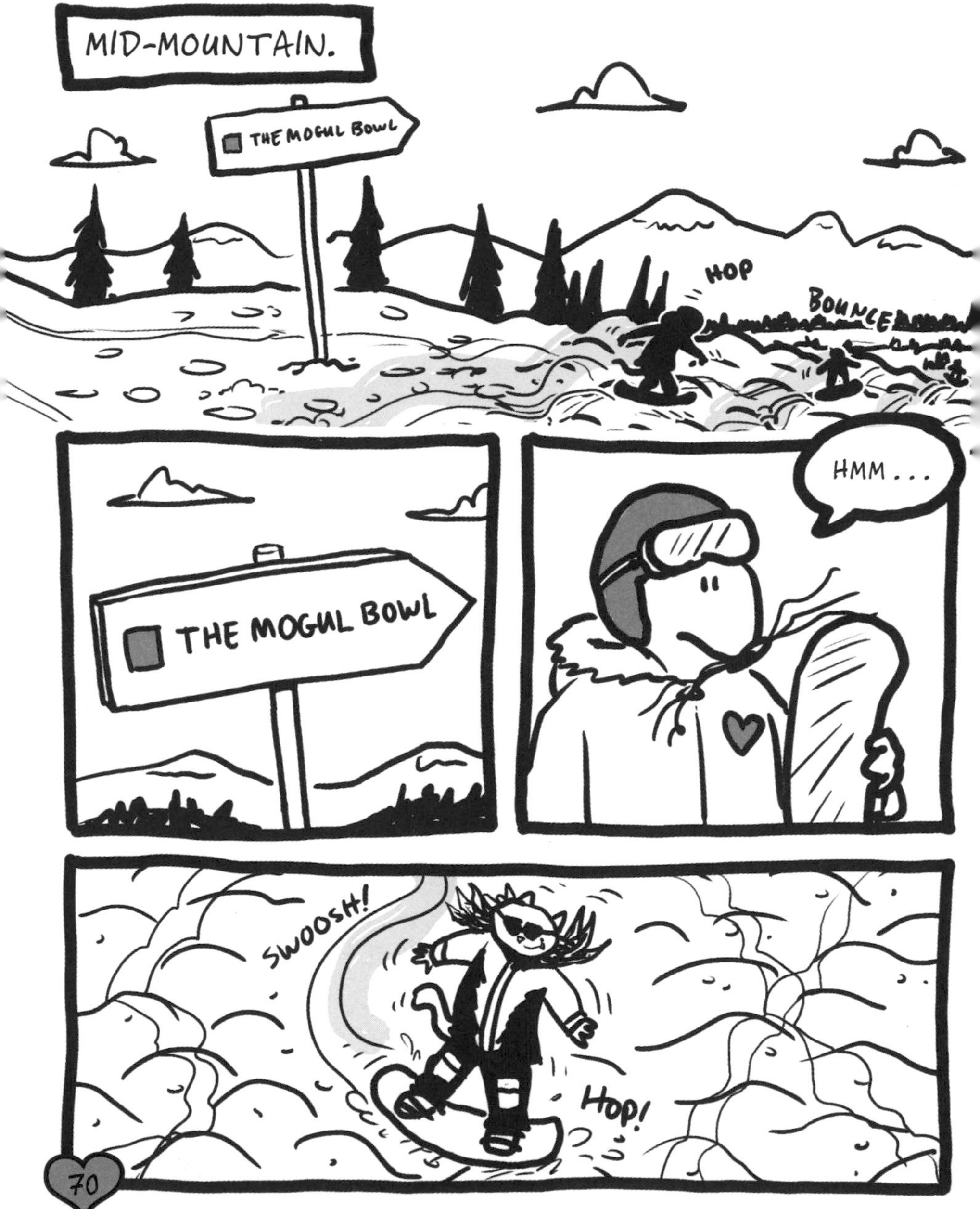
MID-MOUNTAIN.
THE MOGUL BOWL
HOP
BOUNCE
THE MOGUL BOWL
HMM . . .
SWOOSH!
HOP!

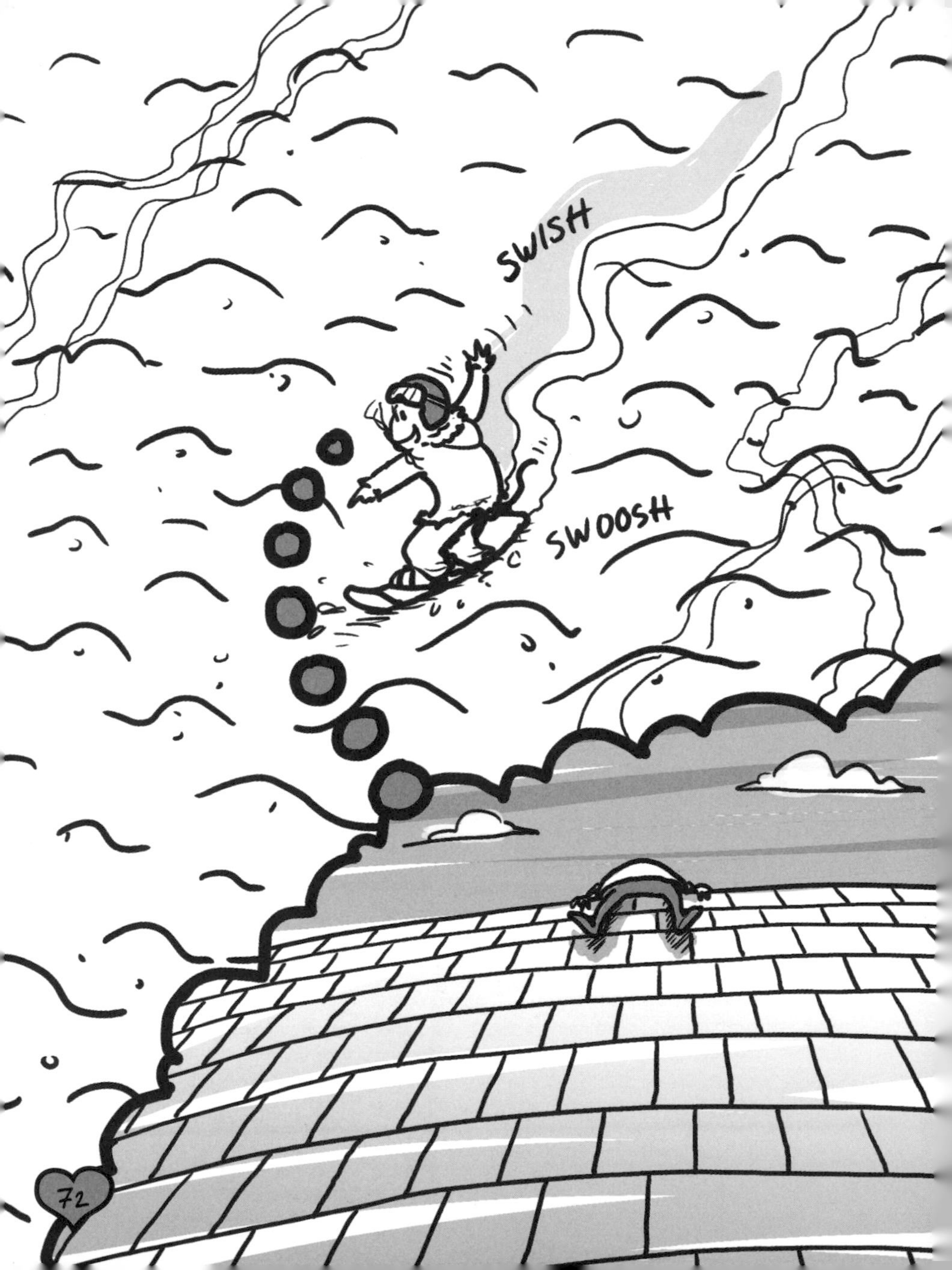
SWISH
SWOOSH

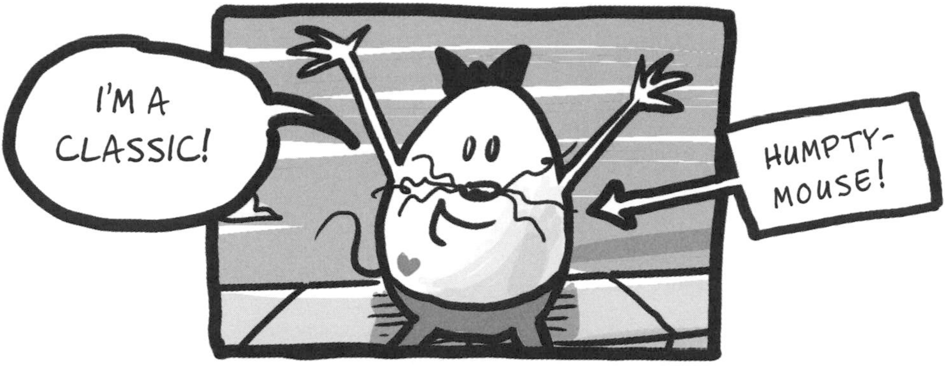
I'M A CLASSIC!
HUMPTY-MOUSE!

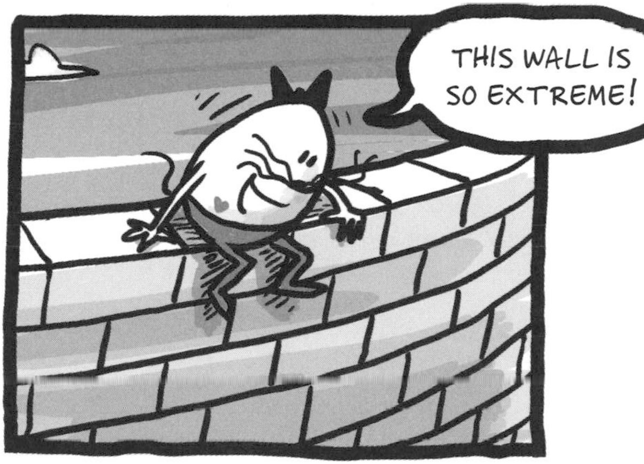
THIS WALL IS SO EXTREME!

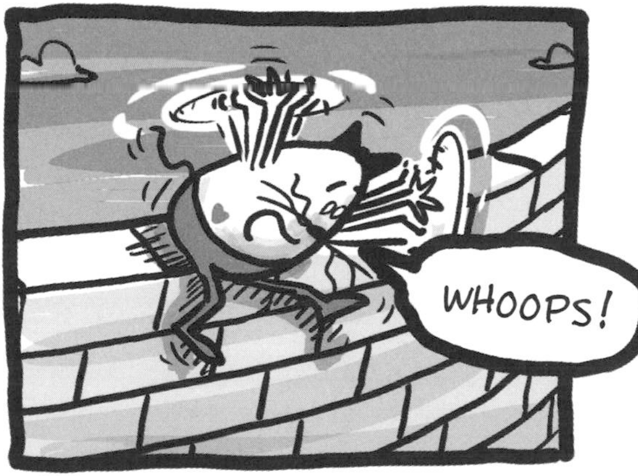
WHOOPS!

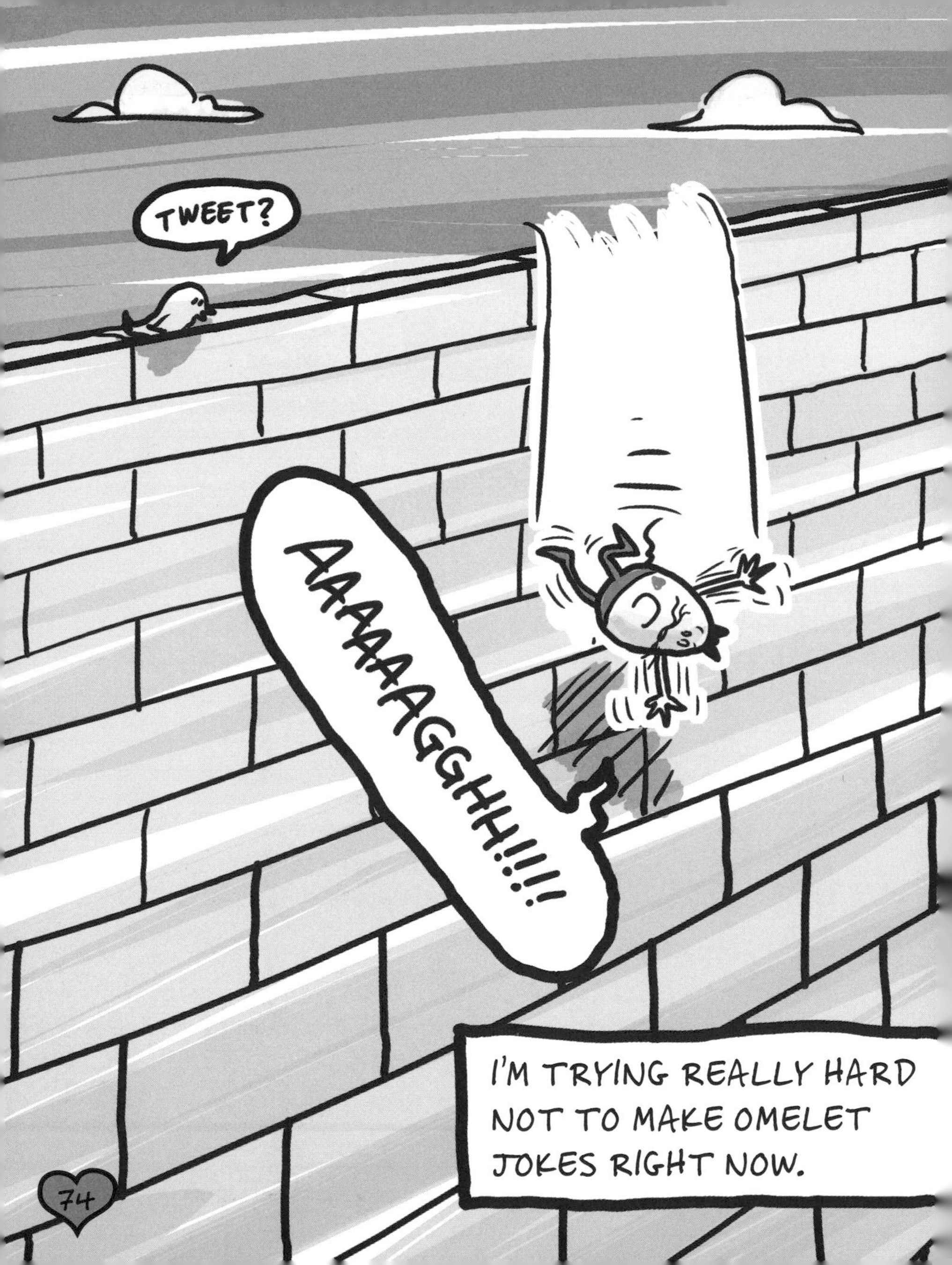
TWEET?
AAAAAAGGHH!!!!!
I'M TRYING REALLY HARD NOT TO MAKE OMELET JOKES RIGHT NOW.

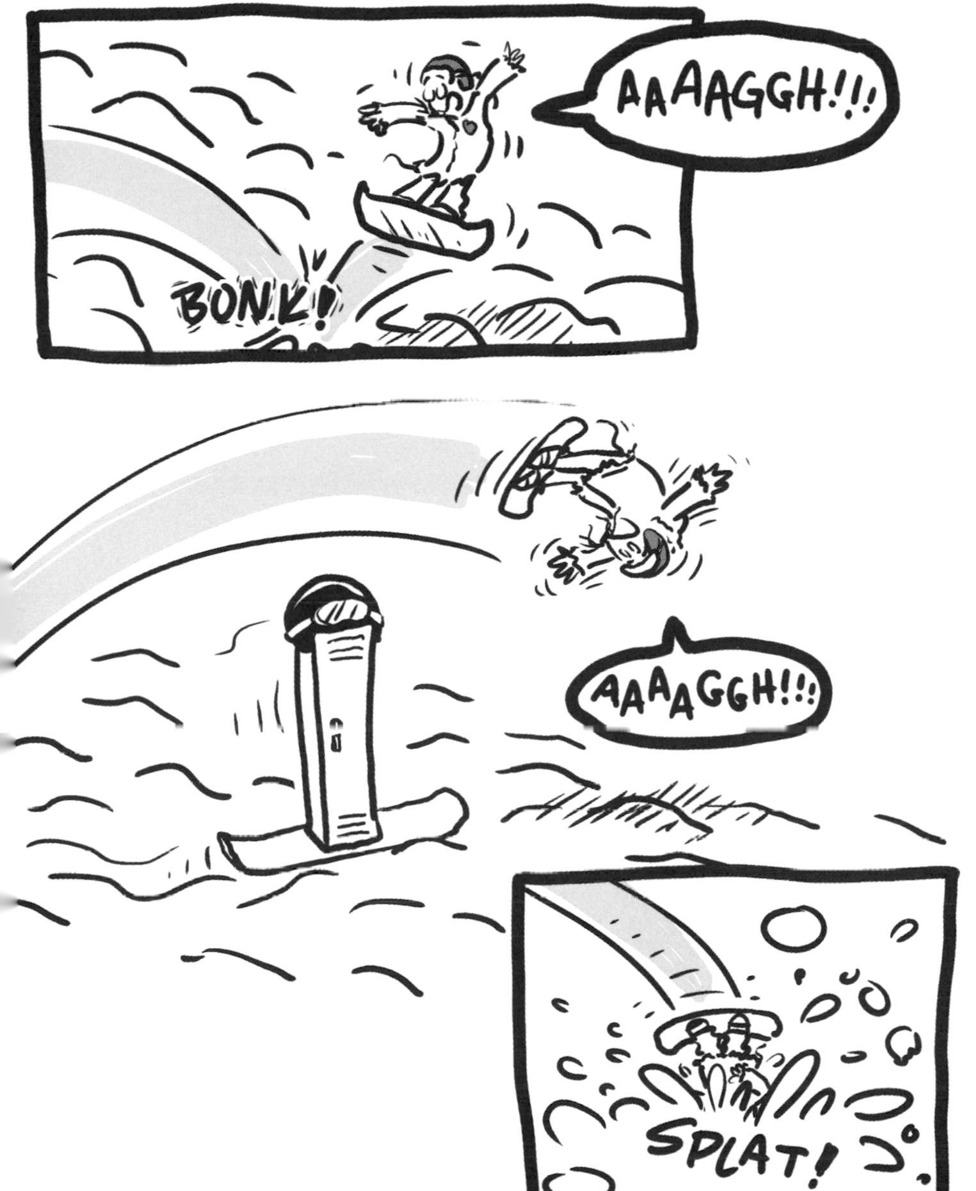
AAAAGGH!!!
BONK!
AAAAGGH!!!
SPLAT!

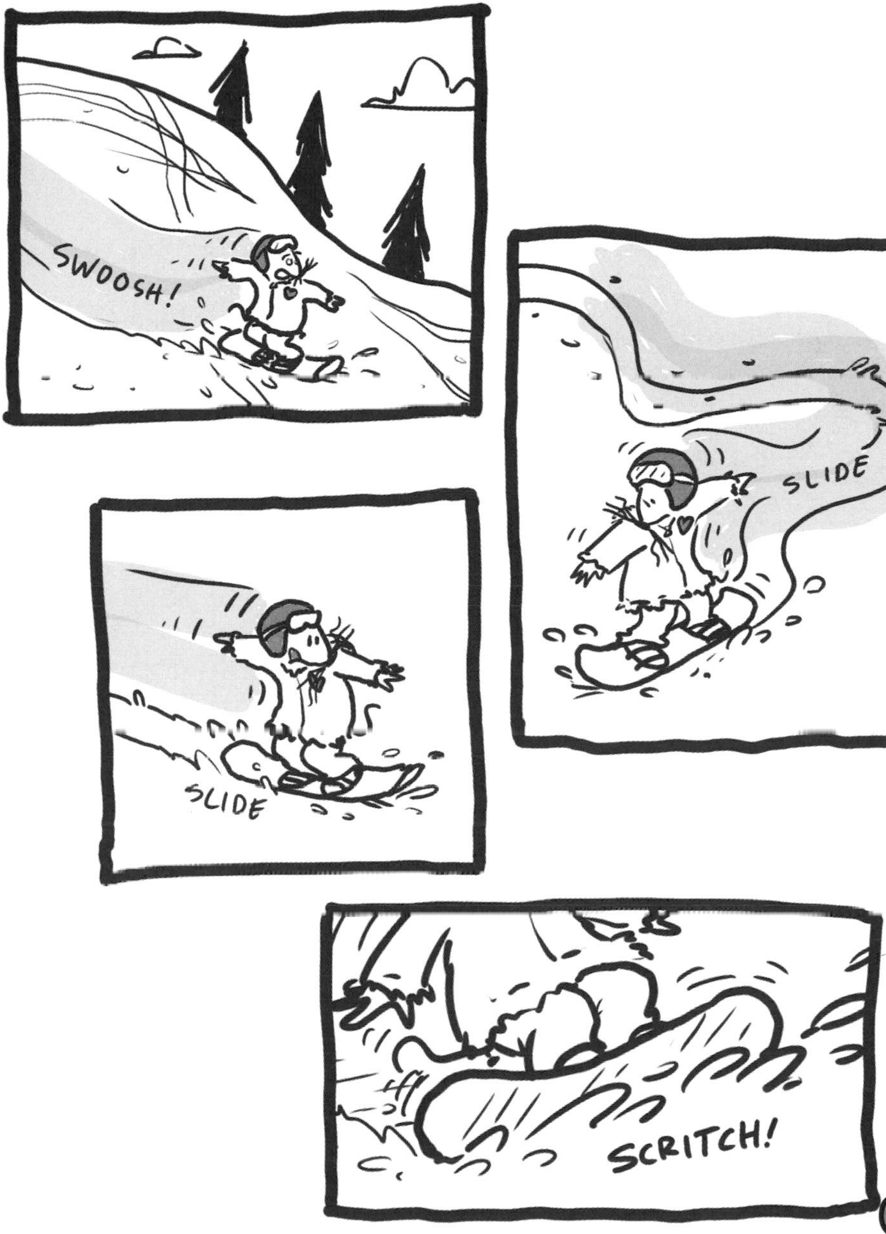
SWOOSH!
SLIDE
SLIDE
SCRITCH!

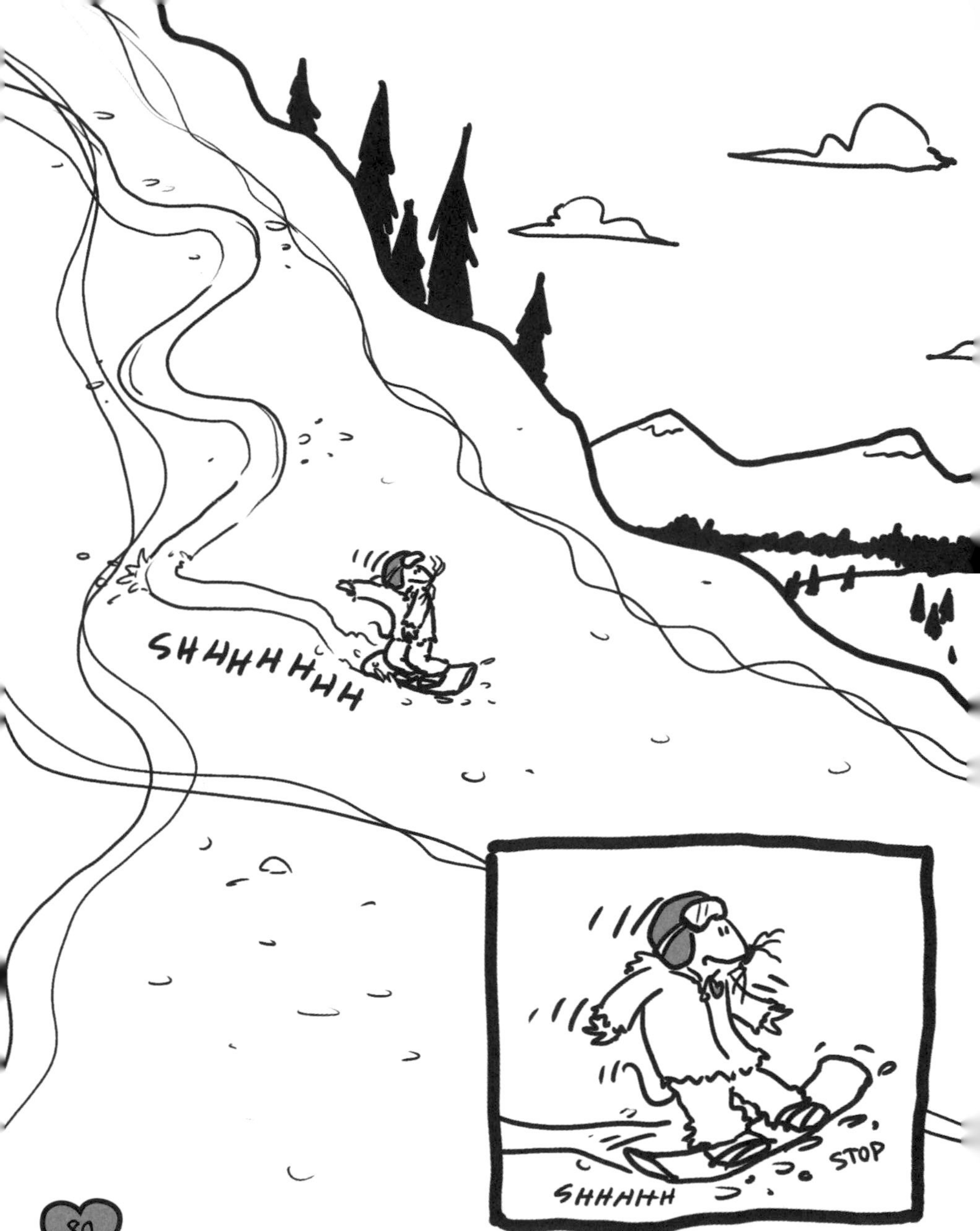
SHHHHHHH
STOP
SHHHHH

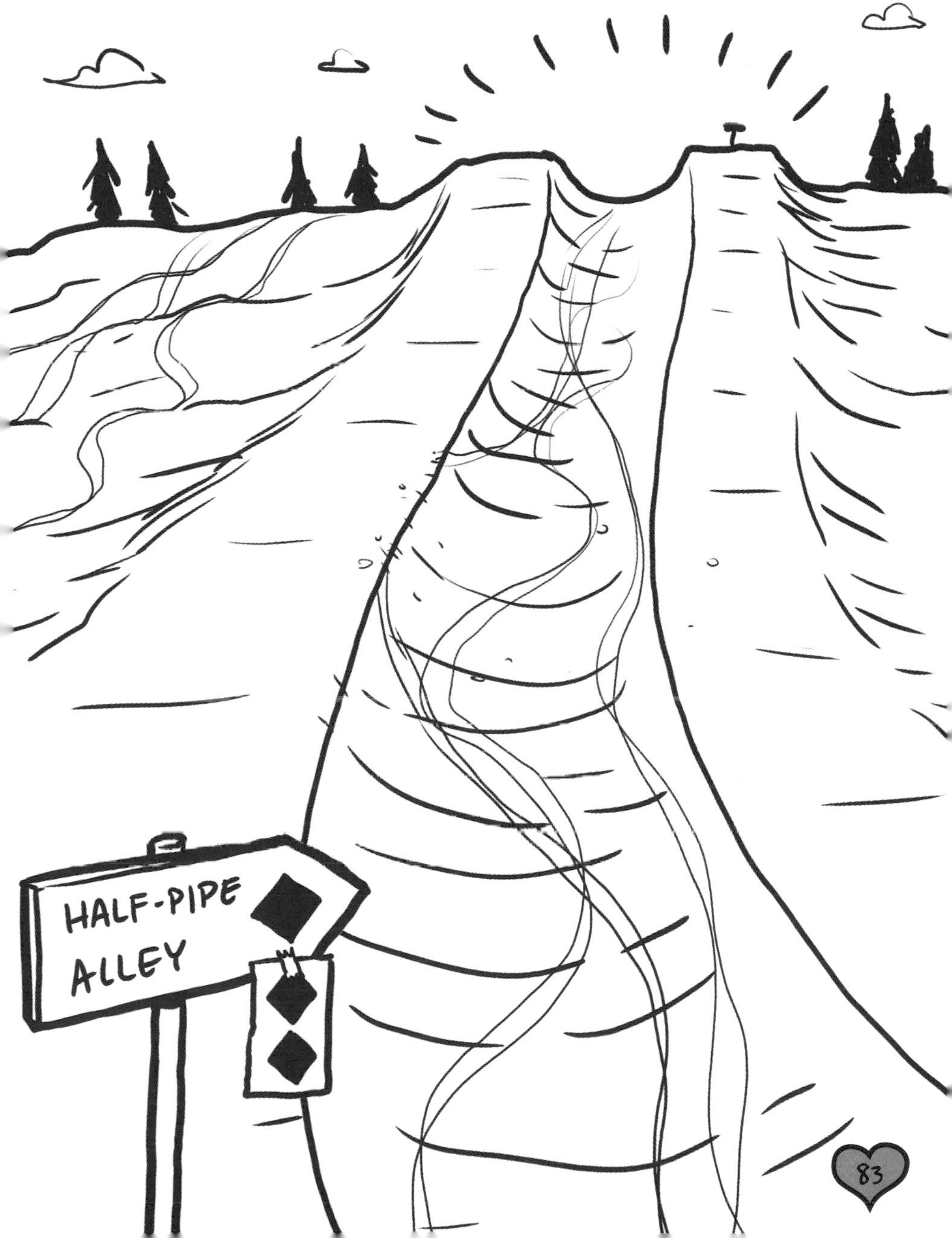
HALF-PIPE
ALLEY

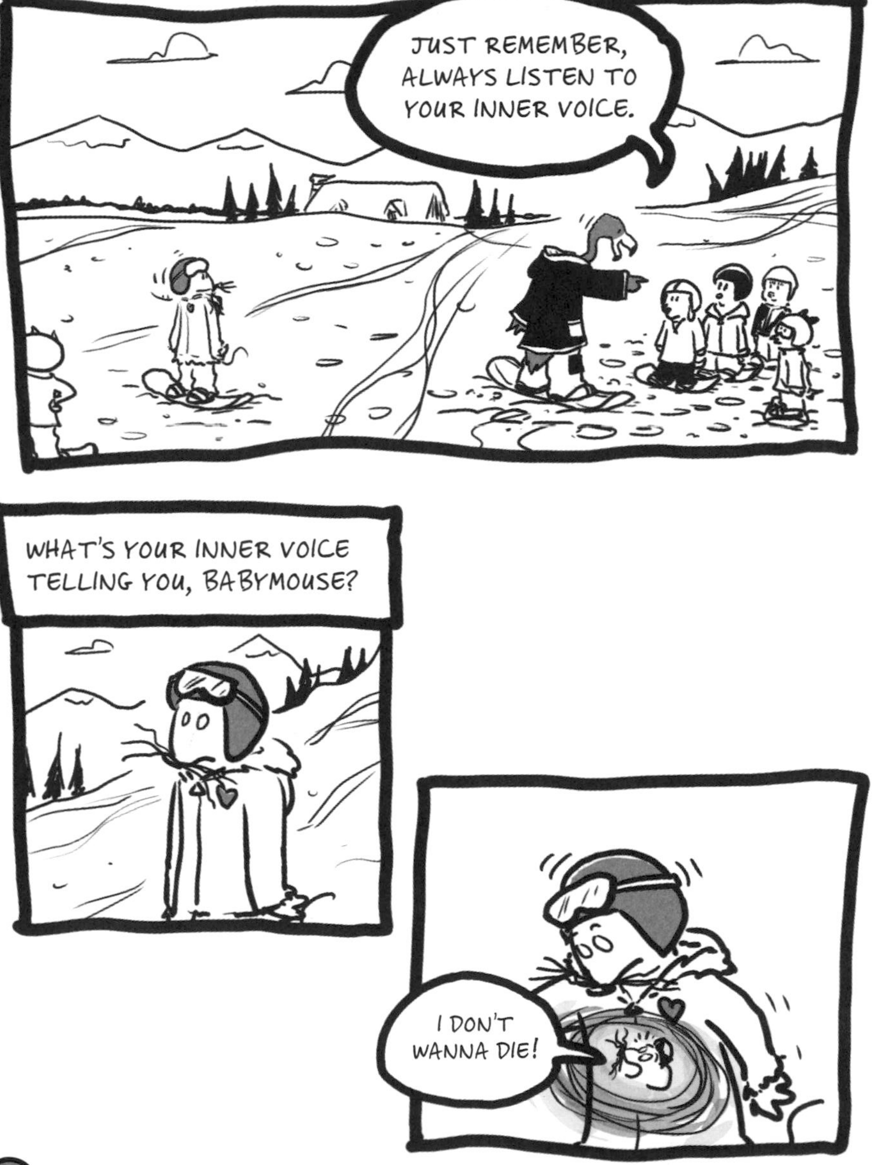
JUST REMEMBER, ALWAYS LISTEN TO YOUR INNER VOICE.
WHAT'S YOUR INNER VOICE TELLING YOU, BABYMOUSE?
I DON'T WANNA DIE!

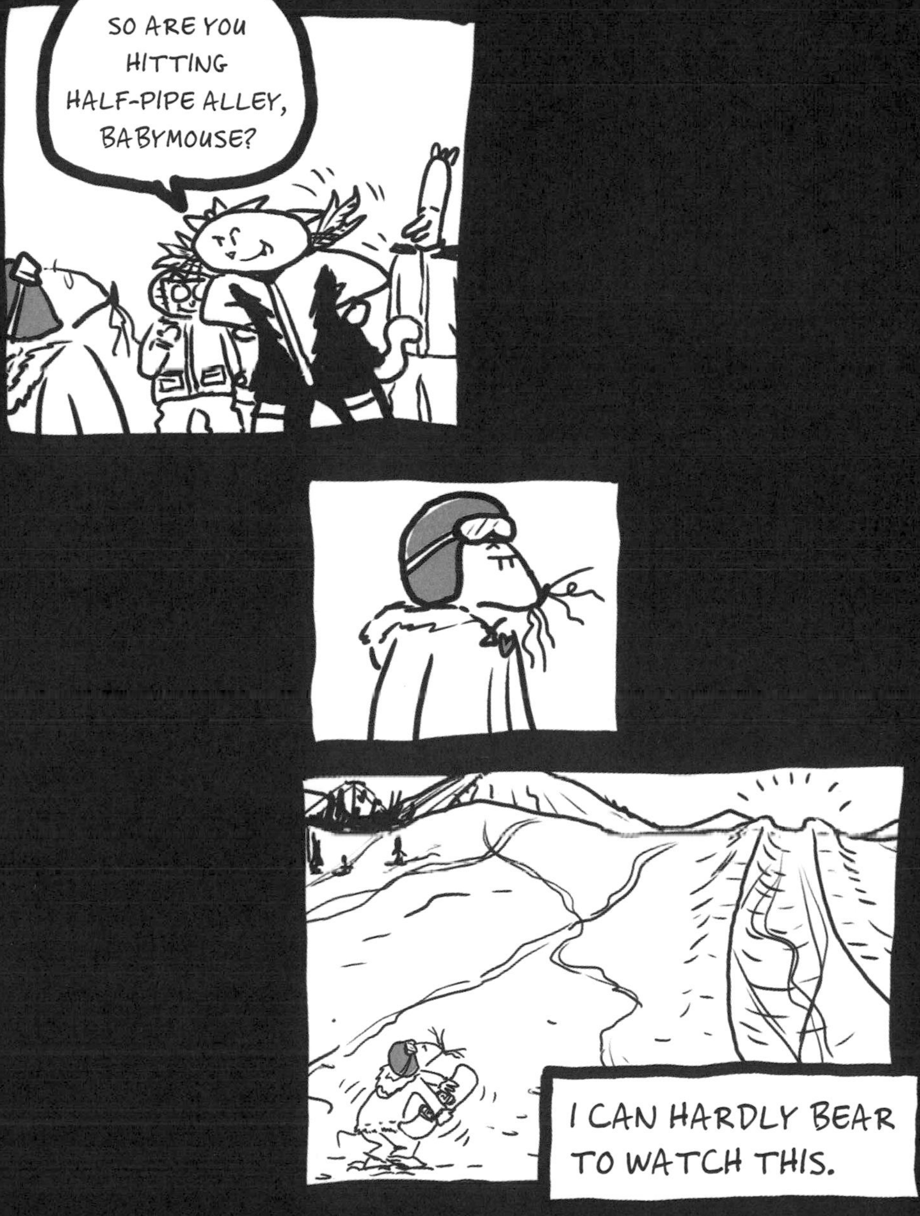
SO ARE YOU HITTING HALF-PIPE ALLEY, BABYMOUSE?
I CAN HARDLY BEAR TO WATCH THIS.

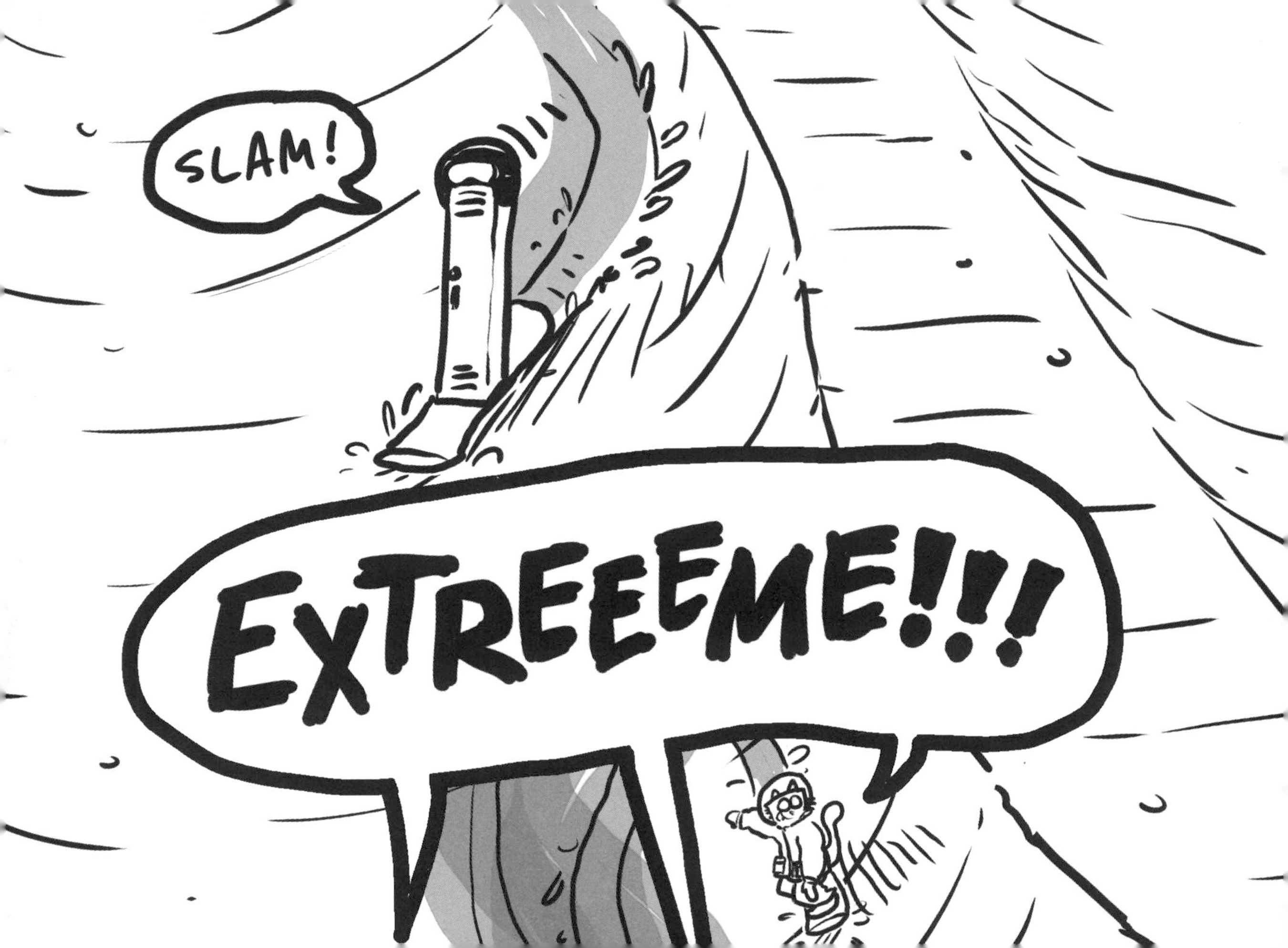
SLAM!
EXTREEEME!!!

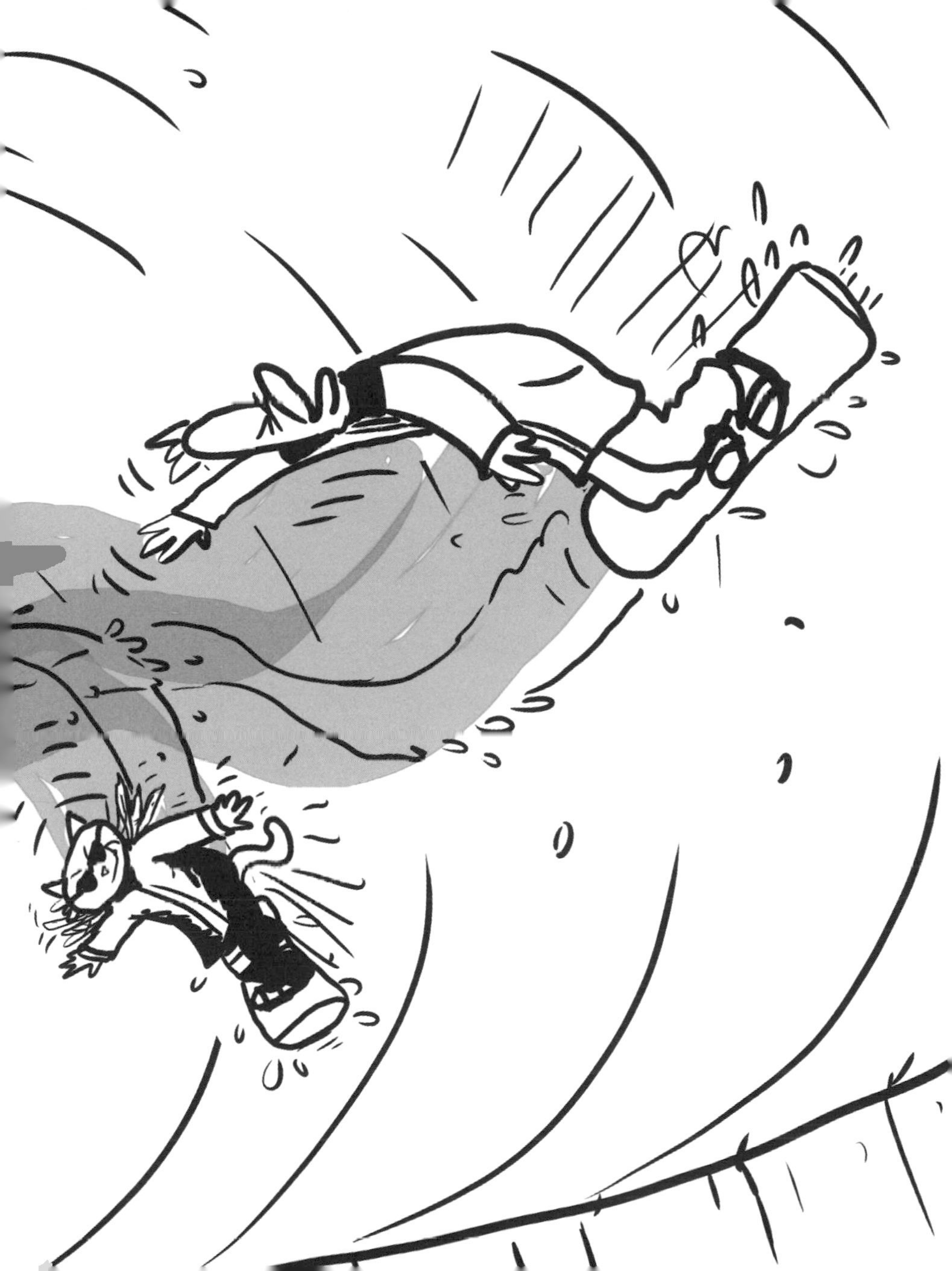

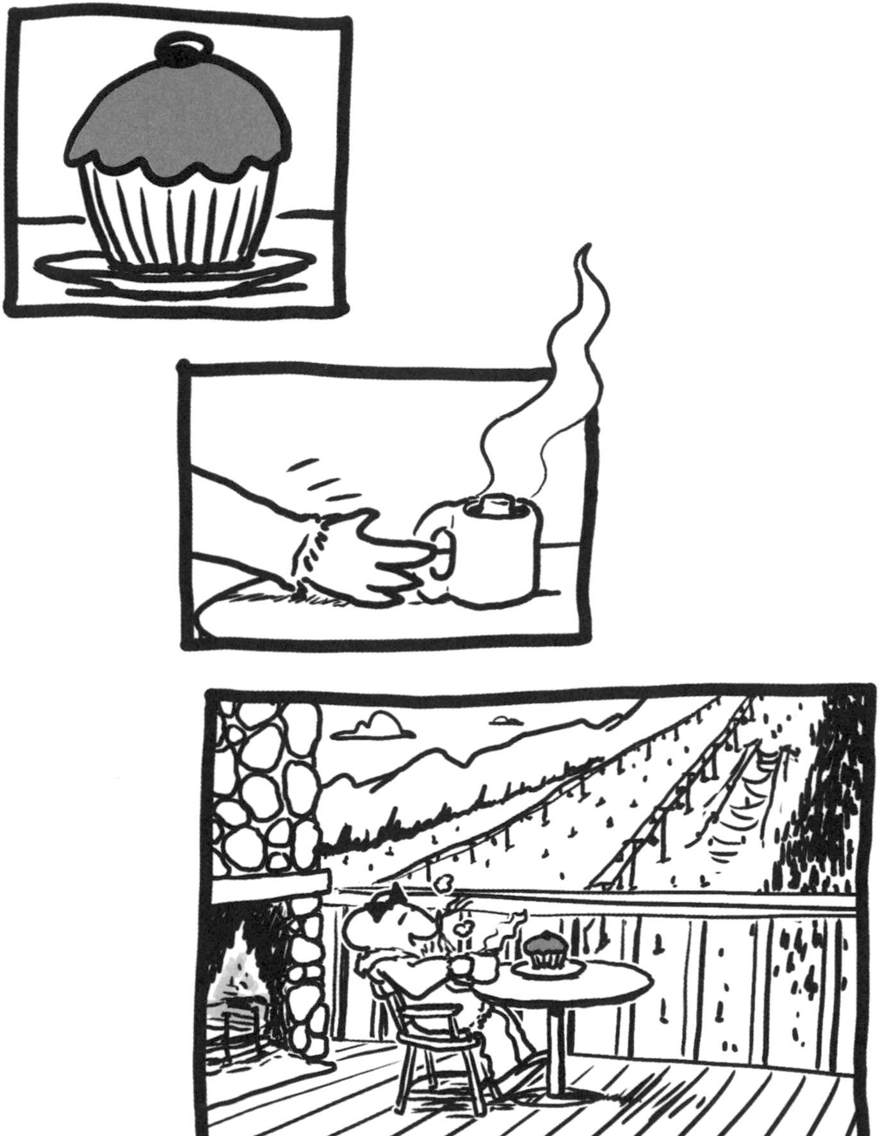

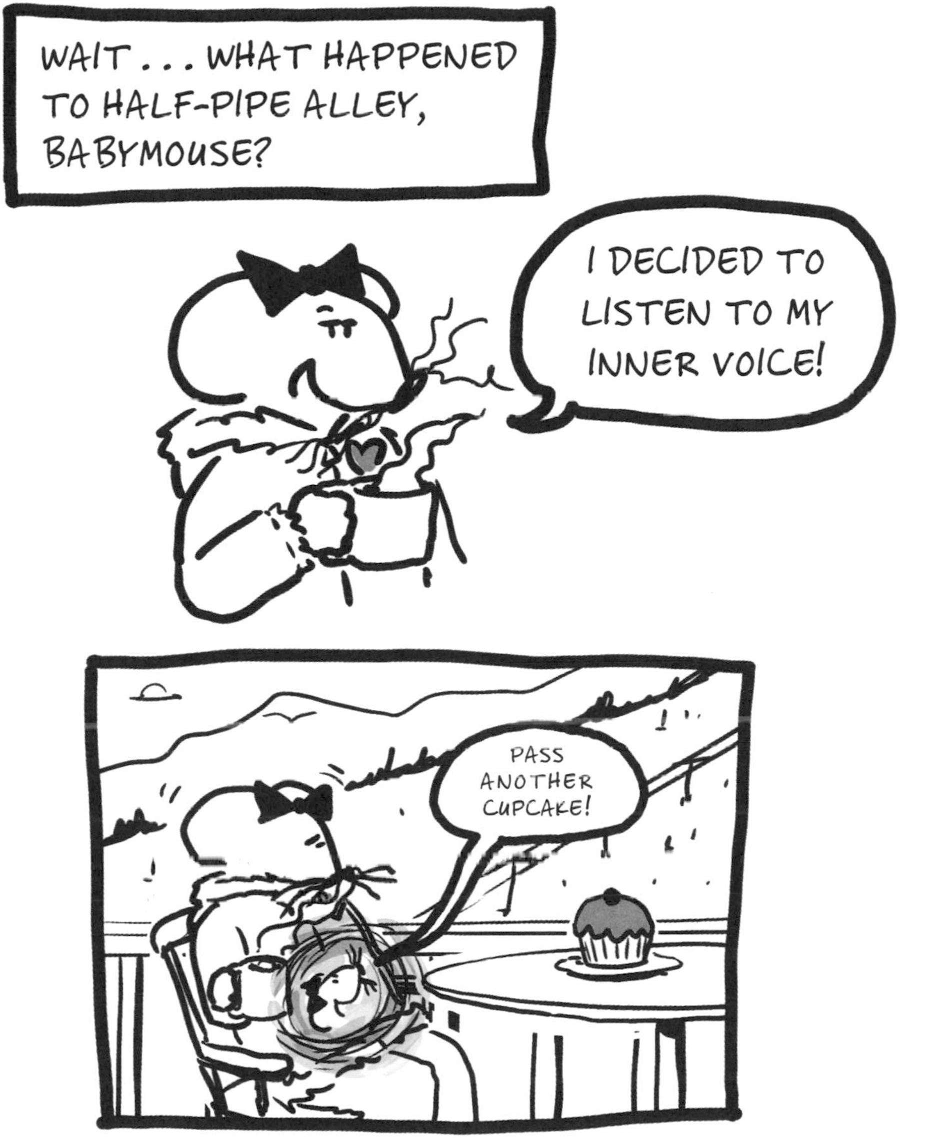
WAIT . . . WHAT HAPPENED TO HALF-PIPE ALLEY, BABYMOUSE?
I DECIDED TO LISTEN TO MY INNER VOICE!
PASS ANOTHER CUPCAKE!

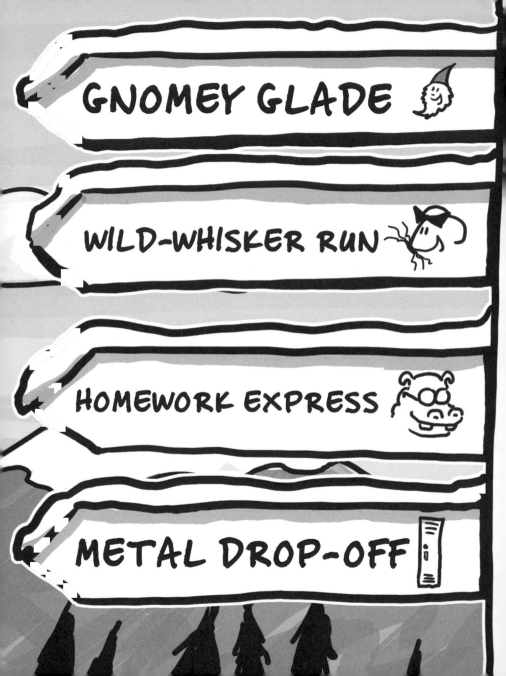

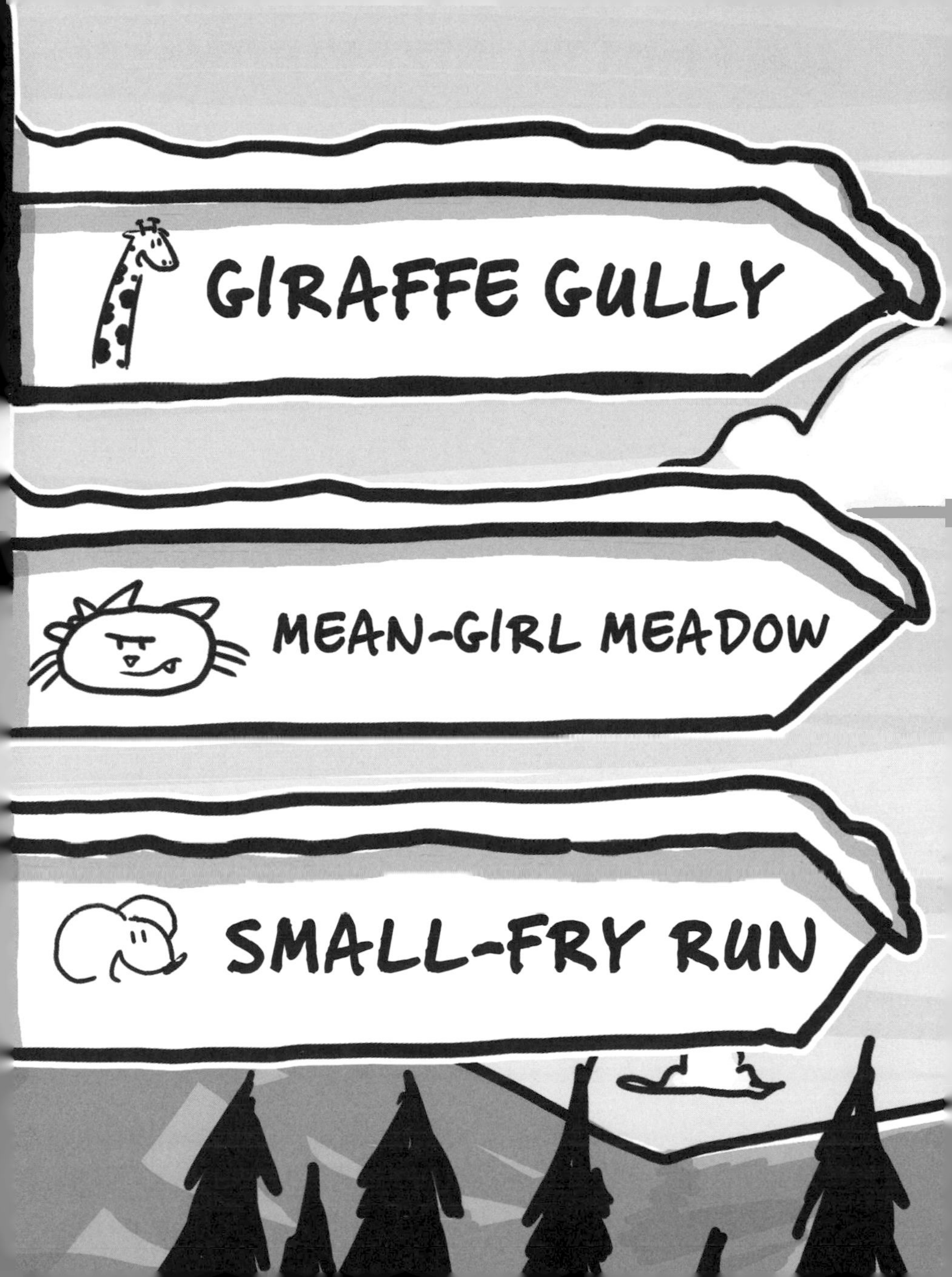
GIRAFFE GULLY
MEAN-GIRL MEADOW
SMALL-FRY RUN

DON'T MISS THE NEXT BABYMOUSE!

HAPPY BIRTHDAY, BABYMOUSE

COMING IN SEPTEMBER 2013

READ ABOUT
SQUISH'S AMAZING ADVENTURES IN:

AND COMING SOON:

★ "IF EVER A NEW SERIES DESERVED TO GO
VIRAL, THIS ONE DOES."
—KIRKUS REVIEWS, STARRED

If you like Babymouse,
you'll love these other great books
by Jennifer L. Holm!

THE BOSTON JANE TRILOGY

EIGHTH GRADE IS MAKING ME SICK

MIDDLE SCHOOL IS WORSE THAN MEATLOAF

OUR ONLY MAY AMELIA

PENNY FROM HEAVEN

TURTLE IN PARADISE

THEY'RE
REALLY GOOD!
TRUST ME!

Walla Walla
County Libraries